You're Lion

From planet Aurora, lioness shifter, Dalissa ____, wants to explore new places before she goes insane from boredom. So a trip to Earth is a must. Finding her mate in the process would be great too, if Gerri Wilder can make it happen. But according to her parents, her smaller than normal size and delicate features make her undesirable to a shifter.

Azai Whittip, alpha of the White Tip wolf pack, will only accept his true mate for a life-long partner, to the dismay of the females in the pack. When Gerri asks him to take her friend sightseeing, he doesn't expect this friend to be gorgeous and smell so damn good. Oh, and bonus, she's his mate.

As far as Azai is concerned, life's perfect now that he found Dalissa. But someone in his pack or the neighboring lion pride think wolves and lions don't mix. When both alphas and the male wolves come up missing, it's up to Dalissa to figure out what's going on and how to stop the one person set on destroying both packs and dominating the human world. Talk about an adventure!

YOU'RE LION TO ME

PARANORMAL DATING AGENCY

NEW YORK TIMES and USA
TODAY BESTSELLING AUTHOR
MILLY TAIDEN

Published By
Latin Goddess Press, Inc.
Winter Springs, FL 32708
http://millytaiden.com

Cover by: Willsin Rowe
Edited by: Tina Winograd
Formatting by: Glowing Moon Designs

— For my readers.
When you find the right one, you'll never feel alone
again!

ONE

Gerri walked into her office and sat at her desk. Out of the corner of her eye, she saw her communicator light up.

Incoming communication, ready. Proceed?

"Yes, computer." Gerri figured it was Zaria calling to check in but could be anyone on planet Aurora. This was the only way they communicated. A moment later, a 3D image popped up of Zaria.

"Hello, Zaria, I have your mail. The only thing important I see is a letter from the management company about your apartment. It appears they have someone interested in subleasing. If you're ready, just have someone pick up your personal belongings and drop off this signed release to their office." Gerri looked

1

up to the screen in front of her. Zaria's smiling face beamed back at her.

"Oh, that would be great. I was actually contacting you today because my friend Dalissa Furr wants to come to Earth, explore, see what shifters are like there and just see my world. You could even look into setting her up or something. She needs a good man in her life. Maybe I can have her drop off the paper and grab anything from my former apartment I might want."

"Dalissa? Yes. A lioness, if I recall correctly. Yes, that would be perfect. I have a friend who I'm sure would be happy to lend a paw, and he would be happy to show her Earth and our local shifters. This will work perfectly."

"I know that smile, Gerri," she exclaimed excitedly. "You're already plotting to set her up, aren't you?"

"Of course. It's what I do best. When should I expect the little lioness to join me? I will take her to your apartment and get that settled before her escort arrives."

"How about tomorrow? I will talk to Dalissa right now and make sure she's good with this. Is that enough time for you to get your plan set up? I mean get your escort on board."

"Don't be cheeky, Zaria. Look how happy you and Quint are. And Bella and Alyx. Should I go on?" Gerri arched an eye at Zaria and waited.

"I'm thankful to you as is Quint. We praise you at least once a day," she giggled. "I was just teasing and having some fun. Thank you for grabbing the mail for me. It should be about done now. Only junk should arrive so the new tenants can deal with it."

"You're welcome, love. Now I must go. I have a lioness to get set up. With an escort, and I mean for town not the other kind. I will meet you at the palace tomorrow morning."

Gerri hung up and sat back in her chair. Now to call in a favor from that pesky wolf. He was going to hate it. Gerri smiled. Oh, yes. This was going to be a lot of fun. She picked up her cell phone.

After a few rings it went to voice mail and Gerri left a message for Azai Whittip. "Azai, it's Gerri Wilder. It's been a while since we spoke, but I need a favor from an old friend. For old times' sake. A friend of mine is coming in from Aurora and I need you to show my friend the sites on Earth and shifters here. It's very different than Aurora. I expect to see you in two days at my apartment. No excuses."

She wished she could see his face as he listened to her message; he would not be happy. He spent a lot of time with her while he was growing up, so she knew he'd never say no to her request. Oh, he would want to, but he wouldn't dare.

* * *

Gerri smiled when she heard her cell ring. She knew who that would be. This was going to be a fun call. "Hello, Azai. I do appreciate you calling me back."

"Gerri, how are you this evening?"

Gerri laughed. She heard the growl in his voice. He wasn't happy, but he was too polite to say anything without the proper greetings first. Well, at least polite to her, not so much with others. He was a bit on the grouchy side.

"Now, that you decided to call me back. I'm doing well. I just need you to do me a favor for a few days. My friend is coming to Earth from Aurora to close up an apartment for another friend. While here, I was hoping you could take some time out of your busy schedule to show Dali your pack. Dali wants to see how shifters act, how they live and all that on Earth. If you could throw in a few Earth sites while you're at it, I would appreciate it."

Gerri grinned, Dali—it was a good nickname. If Azai knew it was a female, he would absolutely refuse.

He mumbled and then sighed. "All right. Fine. I can be there Saturday morning to pick up this Dali. How long is this going on for?"

She picked up a cookie and took a nibble. "Let's play it by ear. No reason to rush. You never know, Dali might be able to help you with your lion issues."

"I assume you aren't going to explain and just be vague as usual? You never change." Gerri pictured Azai in her mind. He was probably banging the back of his head against his chair, with his eyes closed. She couldn't help but let out a small chuckle.

"Nope, but Dali can be your help in any manner of ways. You just have to be willing to give it a shot."

He growled softly. "Good night, Gerri. I have a few things to take care of before I get this Dali from you."

"Lovely to hear from you again. Good night, Azai." Gerri hung up with a satisfied smirk.

TWO

A zai Whittip hung up the phone and slammed it on the table in front of him.

"Whoa, boss, what happened?" He looked up to this best friend and pack beta, Jed.

"Sometimes the past comes calling and you have to answer. Mine just called." Azai hung his head and laughed softly. "I'm sure you heard of Gerri Wilder, of the Paranormal Dating Agency? Well, she's my unofficial aunt. I grew up with her nephew and spent a lot of time hanging around her place. She just called in a favor."

Jed sat across from Azai and stared at him. "Of course, I've heard of her, but I don't understand why you're upset she asked for a favor."

Azai shoved back from his chair and stalked to the front door. "Are you coming? I have stuff to take care of before this Dali shows up."

Jed jumped out of his chair and followed him outside.

"So, a guy named Dali is coming and Ms. Wilder wants you to do what with him? Who is Dali, anyway? Do you have any more information?"

Azai growled his impatience. "Dali is from Aurora. The shifter planet. He's never been to Earth and wants to see how different our shifters are compared to them back home. It's my job to show him around and play nice basically."

"Seems simple enough. I mean, I know it's not great timing. With the pack females trying to get you to pick a mate. Not to mention the issues with the lions." Jed shrugged like it was all no big deal.

He stomped outside, growling. "Exactly. The last thing I want is to escort some random person around. I've got bigger problems than playing tour guide. Unfortunately, with Gerri nothing is as simple or easy as she says. She matches everyone! So, this Dali will be a mate to someone in our pack." Azai growled again.

Fuck! She didn't care if the other person was ready for their mate; she just sent them over and let the cards fall where they may. When he was younger, it used to amuse him but now when it was his pack on the line. Well, that was another story. "You know we should welcome Dali to the pack. Don't you know how to short sheet a bed?"

Jed barked out a laugh and froze in his tracks. "Are you being serious?"

Azai smirked at Jed. "Why the hell not, if he's someone's mate. We can have a little fun and maybe Gerri will think twice next time she asks me to escort someone around."

"Whatever you say, boss, but here comes the daily parade. Smile and play nice." Azai could hear the laughter in Jed's voice and he really wanted to hit him. It was ridiculous the mommas in the pack gallivanted their daughters in front of him every day.

Shit, it appeared the single wolves had joined in too. Why they thought walking in front of him, literally, in a line like a fashion show, would suddenly entice him to pick one he had no idea. It wasn't like his wolf would suddenly sit up and say, "Hey, yesterday we weren't mates, but today you're mine."

Azai tried and failed to keep the grimace off his face as he politely watched the females go by. None held his interest and he had better things to do. Though this daily parade might make Dali find his mate that much faster. Which would get him out of Azai's hair that much faster.

When he suddenly smiled, the female in front of his squealed and started jumping around. Azai looked around trying to figure out what just happened. "I can't believe you picked me. I will make you happy even if we aren't mates. I swear!"

Azai glanced at Jed and then back at the wolf in front of him. "Valerie, I will only take my mate as my partner. I'm sorry, but I won't settle for less than what this pack deserves."

Valerie and the other women stomped off. He could hear them muttering and ignored it. He didn't want to know what they were calling him. Jed waited until they were out of earshot and burst into laughter. "You smiled and she thought you picked her! That's epic. You need to smile more often. She wouldn't have gotten the wrong impression if you weren't such a surly bastard."

Jed had a point, but there was too much going on. The lion pride that moved onto the land next door shouldn't have been a problem. They all were animal and human, so why couldn't they coexist? He hoped it was just settling in problems but two packs of hunters so close together made his hackles rise.

He had to come up with a way to keep the peace and the fighting from escalating. Nothing had happened so far, but words exchanged. The younger wolves were testing the boundaries and soon something would erupt.

"Jed, go set up the guest room for me. I can't ask one of the females because they will think I am inviting them into my bed. Don't forget to short sheet the bed too. I have another idea to set up a welcome for our new guest."

Azai marched off in search of the biggest gossip among his pack. If Dali was out for a mate, then Azai would make sure every eligible female stopped by. This was going to be fun, and he could pass off all the female attention to someone else for once. He had a few minutes before he had to meet the lion alpha to see what today's talks could do.

He headed toward the stream that ran through his land. The females liked to sit on the bank. He was sure he could stop by and spread the word about the eligible new bachelor coming to the pack. He had to assume the women would want a shifter that was bigger, stronger than most they encountered.

THREE

Dalissa ate lunch at the picnic tables in the center of the town square, where most of those who lived in her village ate. Every day it was the same old shit, different day. She longed to travel and see new sites. She was tired of just watching everyone else have adventures and find love. Fuck this!

"Hey, stranger, are you moping again?" Dalissa rolled her eyes at Zaria, then jumped up to hug her.

She said, "I haven't seen you much lately, though the sounds coming from your place have kept most of us away. Is the honeymoon finally over?"

She loved how happy Zaria was, truly, but she was also a little jealous. She wanted to have hot and kinky sex all hours of the night with her own mate. Hell, she'd settle for a one-night stand. The shifters around her thought of her as their little sister. None were her mate, that was for sure.

"Well, I wouldn't say over," she giggled. "But that's not why I'm here. I got a letter from the company who owns my apartment on Earth. They have someone to finish out my lease and want me to get anything I want to keep." She shuffled and gave her a pleading look. "I suggested to Gerri that I ask you to go. She agreed to meet you when you get to Earth and take you over. Then she offered to find you a tour guide so you could see Earth while you're there. What do you think?"

Dalissa leaped toward Zaria and tackle hugged her. "Are you serious? You know this is what I have always wanted. Hell, yes, I will go!"

Zaria laughed and stepped back. "Can you get time off from work?"

"Are you kidding?" Dalissa said. "For this, I'd get time off from anything."

"Great. Grab anything from my apartment that has sentimental value like pictures and stuff like that. I will ask Gerri to open a storage unit for me. You need to pack some clothes. I guarantee nothing in my closet will fit you, girl."

Dalissa glanced down her body. She was a bit shorter than most shifters on Aurora, but she was still taller than Zaria. But Dalissa envied Zaria's curves. Zaria was gorgeous and Dalissa couldn't compare her body to that. She had curves but nothing as beautiful. Shifters liked big woman, maybe that was why they avoided her. She was a big girl but not big enough maybe? Dalissa sighed and shook her head. Those thoughts didn't matter right now. She had more important things, like a trip to Earth!

"I'll grab some clothes. Will my stuff from here stand out too much?" Clothes that morphed to fit your needs weren't available on Earth so she would have to be careful.

"It's not like you will be undressing and dressing in front of people, so you should be fine." Zaria cocked an eyebrow at Dalissa. "And if you do, I want details all about him and what happened."

Dalissa shook her head. "Does Quint know he mated a pervert?" Dalissa hoped she would find her mate, but it was unlikely. Her luck just didn't seem to allow it.

Zaria's smiled faded to her *do as I say* look. "You should call your parents to let them know you'll be gone for a few days. I don't want them freaking out and calling me again because you didn't call them back soon enough."

Dalissa blew out a breath. "I can take care of myself. Why don't they see that?"

Zaria smiled. "Because they love you and don't want you to get hurt."

"But I'm not that little kid anymore," Dalissa said. "I really need to break away. How can any mate take me seriously when my mom constantly calls to make sure I'm safe?"

Dalissa's parents had coddled her too long. They claimed she was fragile because she wasn't the typical shifter. She was too short. She looked too delicate. They didn't care she was as strong or as fast as anyone else. Maybe if she did something to prove to them she was just as good, it would help.

"Come over tomorrow and we'll go to the palace to meet up with Gerri. Thank you for doing this for me. I really appreciate it." Zaria waved and headed back to her place. Dalissa sat on the bench and watched her go.

She really didn't want to make the call to her parents, but there was nothing else to do. After getting approval from her boss to leave, it would only take a few minutes to pack and there was no one else who would care if she disappeared.

She pulled out her com unit and punched in

the code. After a few minutes of no answer on their side, she decided to leave a message. Maybe they would view it and see she was doing well.

"Hey, Mom, Dad. Just wanted to let you know I'm doing great. I'm actually heading to Earth to help a friend out and sightsee. If you want to contact me, you can call Gerri Wilder, the matchmaker. She can reach me. Hope you're well."

Dalissa closed the link and sighed. Nothing would change with them, but she had better things to dwell on. Like her trip to Earth. Oh god, a trip to Earth! She could barely stop herself from bouncing on her heels. So many possibilities, she couldn't decide what she wanted to do or see first.

FOUR

Dalissa was up early the next morning eager to get to Zaria's and on to the palace. She knocked on the door, despite the moans and groans she heard inside, and quickly stepped back, her cheeks flaming. She'd better sit and wait. It might take them a few minutes to climb out of bed and be decent. Yeah, she wasn't envious at all.

As she waited, Dalissa started daydreaming about what she would see on Earth. The colors, the clothes, the buildings. Everything she heard about Earth was so different from Aurora. Her thoughts were interrupted by her com ringing, *Shit! Her parents were calling back!*

"Hello? Dalissa, we got your message." She

heard disapproval and disdain dripping from her mother's voice.

"Yes, I wanted to let you know I wouldn't be around for a little bit." She tried to ignore the hope that filled her, but it happened every time she wanted to do something on her own.

"We forbid you to go to that disgusting planet. It's full of humans and nasty creatures who could easily harm you. You can find someone here to be your mate. There are plenty of shifters willing to overlook your...weaknesses."

Dalissa's hope drained. Her family always made her feel like shit, like she was less than them. She didn't know why she put herself through this time and again. She counted to ten, back and forth, and tried to keep her emotions from erupting, breathing and voice even. The last thing she needed was her mother commenting on that too.

"I'm not going to Earth for a mate. I'm going to help a friend and look around a bit. It's not a big deal. I just want to have an adventure." She watched the 3D image of her mom.

Her mother rolled her eyes and sighed. "Aurora isn't good enough for you then? Now you're better than the shifters here?"

"Moooom," Dalissa said. She knew what

was coming next — the guilt trip.

"Well, you will do whatever you want regardless of what we say. Just know that you are disappointing your parents. We worry so much about you."

Oh brother. What else was new? She had a lifetime of memories where she disappointed her parents. Her tongue hurt from biting it. "It has nothing to do with upsetting you, Mom, but you wouldn't understand."

"No," her mother spat. "You're the one who doesn't understand how difficult it is to have a child that's different. That doesn't measure up." She rubbed a hand on her temple as if the conversation were giving her a headache.

"I'm sorry to have inconvenienced you, Mom. It's a short trip, so I'll call you when I get back."

The line was cut short so quickly, Dalissa was left staring at nothing. She willed herself not to cry. She could handle their disappointment. She was used to it. Fuck! It never got easier to deal with them.

She sat there, her mind consumed with memories of letting her parents down and being told what a disappointment she was. God. She wished she could give herself amnesia.

"Dalissa, I called you three times. Are you

okay?" Dalissa jumped up and spun around, her hand smacking her chest as she took a quick draw of breath to calm her racing heart. "So much for shifter hearing. I almost had a heart attack. I'm sorry. I was thinking about Earth and got lost in my head. Then my mother called and how much of that did you hear?"

Zaria sighed and Dalissa could see tears in her eyes. "I heard more than I like." Zaria leaned in and hugged her, then headed back inside. "You're here early, eager to go on your adventure? Give me a few minutes to get dressed and we can head to the palace. I'm sure Gerri will be here shortly."

Dalissa rocked back and forth on her feet. "Can I ask you some questions about Earth? I want to be prepared. I mean, I know I can eat anything there and all, but still. I'm a bit nervous and so excited." Plus, it was a good way to keep her mind off her conversation with her mother.

Dalissa realized she sounded as timid as the lion her parents thought she was, but this was a huge experience and she was going on her own. What could go wrong with a matchmaker as your guide? Dalissa froze and looked at Zaria. "Holy shit! Is Gerri planning to match me with a human? I mean, that's what she does, or is this purely a favor to you?" Shit, her parents would keel over if they thought she was being set up.

Dalissa watched Zaria's face. "If she set you up, would it be so bad?"

Dalissa frowned. "No, but a human male is never going to be seen as my equal," she sighed. "I'd have to leave him behind on Earth or stay there with him."

Zaria waved a hand as if that wasn't a big deal. "I accused Gerri of setting you up, but I don't know for sure. She's a really lovely woman, so she could just be doing us a favor. She wouldn't match you up with anyone weak, either. Human or shifter. Just go, have a good time and see where fate takes you."

FIVE

Azai practically ran from the women. They were acting like leeches instead of wolves. He really didn't understand why they thought he would take just any female to be his. That place was reserved for one special person, and she better be ready to handle that gaggle of estrogen.

He looked forward to meeting with the lion king, if only to not hear one simpering giggle.

Azai approached the copse of woods they had been meeting at the last two weeks and slowed his steps. Something smelled off. He couldn't place it, but it made him nervous. He heard movement coming from the lion's territory and he stepped out of sight behind a tree to observe who came into the clearing. After a moment, he saw Remy, the lion alpha.

"Remy, I'm here. Watch your step. Something's wrong, but I haven't had a chance to look around yet and see what it is."

Remy sniffed the air and snarled. "You're right. I smell it. Some chemical, strong and harsh in my nose."

They both turned and started walking the area trying to identify what it was. "Azai, come over here. You need to see this."

There was raw anger in Remy's voice. Azai hoped it wasn't trouble caused by his pack.

Burned into the tree in front of Remy were the words *Lions and Wolves, Oh my...*

Azai stared at it for a moment and then walked around the tree to see if there was something they were missing.

"Remy, any idea what could have done that and caused this odor?" Remy frowned and leaned in to sniff the tree closer.

"I can't place what was used, but it's the cause of the odor. What do you think it means?"

Azai didn't see anything on the other side of the tree and moved to look at the ones around it. "I don't know, but my guess is there's more whoever wrote that wanted to say."

Remy nodded and glanced around,

surveying their surroundings and searching for anything strange.

After a few minutes, they met by the first tree. "I didn't see anything else or smell more. What about you?"

"Nothing. Someone's playing a game with us. I don't like it. I don't like not knowing what this shit is about. I definitely don't want it to escalate. Any rumbling about us talking that you heard?"

Azai ran his hands down his face and sighed. "Just the kids we knew about. Nothing new from my wolves. What about you?"

"Same. The younger lions are being assholes, but no one else has said anything. I thought we could get this cleared up soon, but apparently someone wants us to have anything but peace."

He tensed, his shoulders tight with frustration. He'd been working hard to make peace so everyone could get along. Why did there always have to be some jackass looking to fuck up everything for everyone else? "It seems so. How about we take turns with patrols around the area to see if we can figure out who left the message. I have a feeling this isn't the end of it."

Remy nodded and stuck his hand out to Azai. Azai shook it and each turned back to the direction they came from.

"Oh, Remy." Azai rubbed the back of his neck, slightly embarrassed at what he was about to ask. "I'm stuck showing a tourist from out of town around Earth and seeing shifters from here. My honorary aunt is Gerri Wilder and I have a feeling this Dali person has a mate around here. Would you mind helping me mess with him?"

Remy whistled. "Gerri Wilder? Of the PDA? Damn, boy, you've got some good friends." Remy laughed. "What did you have in mind for your guest?"

He shrugged, his lips rising in a slight grin. He shuffled his feet in the leaves on the ground of the woods around him.

"If Dali wants to find his mate, I figured I would have the females up close and personal. Would you mind setting up a little demo with your lionesses?" Azai hoped they didn't get offended, but what better way to help a guy find a mate. Not to mention get Gerri off his back if he helped. Besides, he really wanted to have some fun. Azai glanced around the trees, he was embarrassed and hoping no one was around to hear him.

"You're evil. I'll explain and see what I can get lined up for you. At least old Bertha is always up for a joke, so I can send her over if nothing else." Remy paled a little bit. "She's a scary one."

"You call me evil? I heard rumors about

Bertha. Are you sure it's safe to involve her?"

Remy grinned and waved over his shoulder as he walked away. Azai sighed and headed back to his cabin, a walk in the woods always cleared his head, but not today. He had a few things to take care of before heading to Gerri's place in a couple hours. Starting with food, he was sure the ladies in the pack would be happy to feed them both, but he didn't want to take a chance one would try to drug him and slide into his bed.

Okay, so he was exaggerating, but they would take advantage of any crumb he sent their way. Keeping a distance was the smartest move.

Azai marched into his cabin and straight into the guest room to check it out. He inspected the bed closely to see if he could see any difference. Either Jed didn't do it or it looked completely normal. He smiled to himself and headed to the kitchen to take stock of his inventory. Feeding two shifters would require an abundance of food and his cupboards were quite bare.

SIX

Dalissa walked to the palace grounds with Zaria by her side. "I'm a bit nervous about going to Earth. What if it's nothing like I built it up in my head?"

Beside her Zaria laughed softly. "You've seen videos, right?"

"Yeah, but-"

"Nothing ever lives up to the expectations we have for them. You just have to suck it up and enjoy it for what it is."

Zaria and Dalissa jumped back when Gerri stepped out of trees in front of them. "No need for fear, girls. It's only me. Zaria, that was insightful. But you're quite right." She grinned widely and hugged each of them. "Dalissa, don't worry. You'll love Earth. I found the best possible guide to show you around. Are you ready to begin your adventure?"

Dalissa turned to Zaria and squeezed her hands. "Anything you forgot to tell me? Anything last minute from your apartment?"

Zaria laughed and shook her head at Dalissa.

"Quit stalling," she chided and gave her a quick hug. "I'm sure you will take care of everything. I love you, girl, now go see my world and enjoy it."

Dalissa turned to Gerri. "Do I need to hold your hand or something?"

Behind her, she could hear Zaria laughing.

"Not unless you want to, of course. Just step through the portal with me and you will be on Earth." Gerri's smile soothed some of her anxiety. Nothing to it. Just step in and go to another world. Shit, this was creepy and exciting.

Dalissa smiled over her shoulder at Zaria and stepped through with Gerri. The air moved around her and suddenly she was in a room, staring at a wood door and gray walls. A screeching and deep thumping vibrated her body. "Well, this is interesting. Gerri, are we on Earth? Is it always this loud?"

She was confused. They had transported into

some type of room with a constant humming noise. Was all of Earth like this? Where the hell was she? She spun in a circle inspecting every inch of the room they stood in.

"The power for the portal is hard to hide on Earth so it's in a power plant. I have a room with my name on it. I'm sure the human employees are confused as hell, but that's part of the fun."

Gerri headed for the door and Dalissa followed, eager to see the rest of the place they landed in.

"A power plant is not the best representation of Earth, but it suits our needs. Just keep following me and you will see your first glimpse of the sky. Unlike Aurora, Earth's is a beautiful blue with pillow thick clouds."

Dalissa craned her neck back and forth trying to see as much of the power plant as she could as they walked. Gerri stepped into a box and smiled at her. "Come inside. It's an elevator. I'm sure you've seen it in Earth movies. It'll take us to the higher floors so we can leave the building."

Seeing something in a movie was another story than living it. Her nerves started to get the best of her. Bile hit the back of her throat. Maybe this trip wasn't all she'd hoped. Shifters weren't meant to be in boxes.

She eyed the elevator warily. It was small. In Aurora, they traveled by all manners of technology, but never a metal box like this. Fuck it. She stepped in and spun around as the doors shut behind her. She stared at her reflection in the shiny metal and gasped when the box moved quickly.

A couple moments later, the doors opened again. She rushed out and glanced around.

She couldn't explain what she saw. Disappointed they were still inside, she sighed. Where were all the people? The buildings? The lights and colors?

She was eager to get out and see everything. Gerri kept walking and she eagerly followed. When they got to another door, Gerri turned to her. "I'll let you do the honors."

Dalissa pushed open the door and walked out. A gasp fell from her lips. "Shit, they weren't kidding," she said in awe. "So much green! I don't know why I didn't believe them when they said everything was green. I always thought the movies were retouched, but it's so pretty."

Across from the power plant, she saw trees and grass. Then she looked up at the sky.

"Oh my god, Gerri. The sky is blue. You said it, but I didn't believe it. And the sun's yellow?" She stared up at the sky, her body vibrating from all the excitement. "Wait, how many moons do they have and what color is it?"

Gerri laughed and hugged Dalissa to her side, squeezing her arm. "You're a delight. You're making me see everything as if for the first time. It's refreshing. But we should head to Zaria's apartment before people begin to wonder why you're gawking around. Plenty to see on the way."

She nodded, her smile unwavering. "Good point. So, when do I meet this guide who will be showing me around the area?"

Dalissa was getting a sore neck from the constant swiveling she was doing. Earth had so much to see, so little of it was nature! She was in awe of how much city they could pack into a small area.

The air was different. Metallic. She wondered what Gerri had planned and what she was going to see.

"Azai is the alpha of the White Tip Pack. He's going to show you his land so you can see shifters here and how they interact. Things are a bit different than back home. He grew up with my nephew and was around constantly, so I called in a family friend favor." Gerri smirked as she said the last part.

Dalissa figured that meant he wasn't happy

about it but would do it anyway. She sighed and ignored it for now. There was too much to see and do to worry. Gerri waved to a car and it stopped next to them. She opened the door and gestured for Dalissa to climb in.

"You want me to get in this thing? Is it safe? I think I prefer our transportation at home."

Gerri's tinkling laugh sprinkled the air. "It's safe. It's just a car and similar to our bikes at home. We just travel on the ground here versus hovering above it."

Dalissa glanced around and then climbed in. She was surprised to find the seat comfortable. After a few moments, she forgot her fear and enjoyed the view from the passing scenery.

Sooner than she would've liked, they were at Zaria's place. It didn't take much time to collect her friend's things.

"That was kind of weird. I mean going through Zaria's apartment kinda felt like invading her privacy. I'm glad it's done though." Dalissa stared at Gerri's apartment building as they walked up to it. "So, this is where you live? Earth is really different, but I am enjoying it so far." A chill traveled up Dalissa's spine. She felt as if someone was watching her. Ridiculous. So few even knew she was coming.

They didn't have apartments on Aurora, so

the concept was interesting but scary too. Who would want that much metal and material over their heads all the time? Did they not crave the sunshine and fresh air?

Gerri led the way into her apartment unit. "Feel free to look around. I'm going to make a cup of tea. Would you like one?"

Gerri headed into the kitchen and Dalissa looked around the room then replied, "I would love one, thank you."

She walked down the hall and explored Gerri's bedroom, and then into the bathroom. She was curious how different it was on Earth.

"It's weird that nothing changes to suit my needs. I think I would miss that the most." For the most part, the building was similar to what she found on her planet.

She walked around trailing her hands across every surface. She wasn't sure if Gerri could hear her, but talking to herself was completely acceptable. She wandered into Gerri's office and looked around. This was the place that started so many romances.

"Gerri, do you have a running tally of the couples you have matched? I expected to see a wall that looked like a family tree. Matching who with who." She laughed at herself. That was an image and eventually would take up the whole room! She heard a knock at the door and rushed into the living room.

Gerri wasn't in the kitchen, so she decided to answer the door for her. She swung it open and froze in place. Thankfully, she had the door to hang onto.

SEVEN

Azai approached Gerri's door and tried to wipe the frown off his face. He didn't want to come across as a complete asshole. Well, not right away, at least. He knocked and waited. He was impatient to get back to his land and find which ass wipe had left the message on the tree.

He rocked from foot to foot and glanced around the hallway at the other apartments. A soft growl left the back of his throat. He didn't have the time or patience to deal with anything else right now, but a promise was a promise.

The door swung open and a scent he wasn't prepared for hit him.

Mate!

Mate!

Mate!

His wolf roared loudly, pushing at his skin. For fuck's sake! He really didn't need that shit. He groaned internally. He'd known Gerri was up to something! He cleared his throat. "I'm supposed to be meeting Gerri today. Is she available?"

A beautiful female hung onto the door like it was a lifeline.

Mine.

Azai stared into the brownest eyes he had ever seen. Was it the mate bond reaching out that had him so mesmerized or was it the stunning face attached to his mate? He was glad he was able to speak clearly and not stutter like an idiot. Good fucking luck trying to sound like an alpha when his wolf was smitten little a pup.

"You must be Azai? Gerri mentioned you would be coming by." The woman stepped back and gestured for him to come in. He walked by and sniffed the air where she'd just stood.

"Yes. I'm meeting someone today. Are you her new assistant?" Azai was starting to put two and two together and it equaled stupid. He was stupid for not realizing Gerri was setting him up to meet his mate. His gut knotted. Oh, no. Dali was short for something.

Azai watched her swing the door shut. Her

scent was full on cherries and cream and made his wolf want to howl. He wanted to press her body against the door and greet her properly.

"Nope," she grinned, her smile dazzling. "I'm in town for a little bit. Gerri is making tea." She glanced around, a small frown on her adorable face. God. He really had turned into a fucking teenager. "I'm not sure where she went. I can look for her."

She left the room and he groaned. Damn that walk was enough to make him drop to his knees in supplication. What he really wanted was to ask who in their right mind was supposed to fight the delicious beckoning of her scent?

The longer he looked at her, the less upset he was at the manipulation. He could only hope her brain was as sexy as the rest of her. Then again, he was already in lust, love couldn't be far behind. He was so fucked. He grumbled his way over to the couch and sat. Shit, thinking about love already.

Mates really screwed with your head. He groaned and leaned back against the cushion. Five minutes in her presence and he was panting after her.

The door to the apartment opened and Gerri walked in, a smile on her face and an evil twinkle in her eyes. He wondered if Gerri had demon blood because she was pure evil.

"Good afternoon, Azai. I've missed you." Her voice was light and full of laughter.

Azai hugged Gerri. "Missed me?" He snorted. "Only you would say that about my growly ass. Why do I think you're trying to butter me up? I already met your house guest. Do I presume that is Dali?"

Azai thought back over the conversation and realized Gerri never once used a pronoun. He assumed based on the name alone. Heat crept up his neck. Damn, he couldn't even be mad at her. She didn't lie, just left out a small detail. He was a goddamned idiot for not being on to her. He paced the living room and watched for Dali to come back into the room. She was gone too long.

"Oh good. I hope you didn't growl at Dali. She's only met a handful of shifters from Earth and they are all women." Gerri scanned the room and then cocked an eye at Azai. Gerri stood in front of him to interrupt his pacing.

"She went to find you. Though, I think she was running more than anything." It wasn't like he'd been an ogre. He'd been polite, but he had stared at her intensely. Like a love-struck fool or one of those creeps from the murder channel. Good luck trying to change that impression.

He hadn't been expecting the punch of attraction as soon as he found her. He knew everyone said the mate attraction was instant, but he thought you still had to build up to the good stuff.

Well, now he knew. He didn't. That was not the case. He was willing to do anything to be with her and that frustrated him. He rocked to the side and tried to see his mate in the kitchen.

Gerri turned to the kitchen when Dali walked out carrying a tray.

"Oh, there you are, Gerri. You disappeared so I finished the tea. The little cakes you had set out look amazing."

Azai tried not to stare at her every move but he was like a moth to the flame and he was willing to die if it meant he was caught in her web. He followed her across the room to the coffee table and hovered behind her.

I don't want her.

You do.

I don't need a mate.

Who gives a fuck? She's yours.

Yes. She was all his. Only his.

"Sorry, dear. Just remembered I had a quick errand. Thank you for the tea and letting Azai in. He tells me he introduced himself." Azai watched as she nodded and looked at him. Gerri's smirk should have annoyed him, but he was too busy keeping his animal in check to think about that.

"I didn't catch your name though. Gerri told me Dali was coming. You weren't what I expected." Azai frowned at Gerri. Her grinning was ticking him off; she didn't appear the least repentant for her behavior.

Dali put the tray down and straightened. "I'm Dalissa," she said in that honey-coated voice. Her smile lit up her eyes making the brown sparkle. Yeah, he was really screwed. "It's very nice to meet you."

Azai reached out to shake her hand. He really wanted to feel her skin against his.

"Dali is short for Dalissa?" Azai tried not to laugh as he watched the confusion play out across her face.

"Uh, yes."

He grinned widely at his mate. His wolf entirely in agreement that they'd keep her close. "Gerri told me her friend was Dali. I naturally assumed a male. I admit I'm much happier with you."

Dalissa grasped his hand and he swore it was as cliché as they said in movies, but fireworks sparked overhead. Christ! Why hadn't someone warned him about this? He wasn't sure how long they held hands or stared at each other, but Gerri cleared her throat and broke their trance. He wanted to push her onto the couch behind them and just hold her close.

"Yes, I thought Dali fit our Dalissa and a bit of subterfuge is never a bad thing in my line of work."

Azai reluctantly let go of Dalissa's hand and stepped back. His hands itched to touch her again.

"Well, now I understand why you said Dali could help me with my lion issues. My pack, on the other hand, may have a few issues." Azai could imagine what the wolves were going to say.

Dalissa wasn't saying much either for that matter. He looked at her again and tried to decipher her facial expressions. Was she dismayed he was a wolf? Was she upset he was not from Aurora? He really wished she would say something and ease his mind. The more he thought about it, the more anxious his wolf got.

"Do you want to sit or just stare at each other?" The laughter in Gerri's voice made him swear under his breath.

Dalissa sat on the couch and he rushed to sit next to her. He must've looked like an idiot, but he wanted to be close to her. His animal approved.

"What lion issues do you have, Azai?" Dalissa asked, her voice flinty sexy. His cock reminded him he hadn't had sex in too long and now that he found his mate, it was great time to come out of his self-inflicted abstinence.

Finally! She was interested so maybe not upset at the match, just overwhelmed?

"A lion pride moved onto the land next to mine. The alpha or pride leader, Remy, and I have been meeting and things are going well, except some of the younger animals are causing trouble." Azai trailed off, thinking about the message on the tree. "Actually, at our last meeting, we found an odd message carved into a tree with chemicals. We aren't sure what it means or who left it. The scent of whomever had been there was covered by whatever they used."

The message and her body heat next to him scrambled his thoughts.

"That definitely doesn't sound good. If there is anything I can help with, let me know. I wouldn't mind a meeting with Remy either. About this problem, of course."

He tried not to laugh out loud and by the look on Dalissa's face. He didn't feel so bad anymore. She was having the same problem he was.

This would be an interesting couple days.

EIGHT

When Dalissa opened the door and saw pure sex standing in front of her, she swore her brain malfunctioned. She wasn't even sure if she remembered how to speak and if she did, was she drooling? She gripped the door and held on.

Holy mother of hot sex on a stick. She'd died and gone to hot-earth-man heaven. The man was so hot, he made her eyebrows sweat. Hot damn! Even her knees were jelly.

He said Dali. Who the hell was Dali?

Then it dawned on her. Oh, damn, that crafty woman set them up. Go, Gerri! Her inner lioness yipped in happiness. After taking a gazillion breaths and calming her excitement and fear, she escaped to the kitchen. Hopefully she could keep her claws off him long enough to learn his name.

She could barely keep herself from dry humping his leg. His scent wafted through the apartment and she moaned. Good lord, this was going to be an exercise in futility. He was hers and nothing would stop her from claiming him.

After a few minutes, she heard Gerri enter the apartment, so she quickly gathered the tea cups. She needed an excuse for running away from him so fast. She could hear him pacing the living room and she couldn't help but smile. Show time.

Listening to him poke fun at Gerri was entertaining, and she kinda liked the nickname. She might have to keep that, or he could use it as a new pet name. Oh yeah, her lion liked the idea of a pet name. She would have to come up with something for her wolf. She blinked. That sounded so odd! Not a thought she ever expected to have!

"Azai, you didn't say what the message was on the tree." He turned his golden eyes to her, and she forgot for a moment what she asked him.

"It said Lions and Wolves, Oh my." She listened to him speak and felt the strongest pull to lean into his body. Thankfully Gerri's smirk kept her firmly on her cushion. But she swore the cushion was sinking and she was falling, right into his lap. That wouldn't be bad, right?

Uh…She quickly straightened and focused on his lips as he spoke.

"Sounds like a play on the song Dorothy, the tin man, and cowardly lion sing in that movie. Lions, Tigers, Bears, Oh My. Do you think there is some kind of reference in there?" Gerri asked, her lips pressed into a frown.

Dalissa didn't know what movie they were talking about, but it sounded like a threat to the pride and pack in her opinion. *Focus on their words and not shoving him down on the couch.* Right.

"I don't know the reference, but it seems like something both groups need to work together on. It's a threat to both of you."

Gerri nodded and Azai stared at her. Just because he made her feel like she was incapable of speech, didn't mean she was. She would like to climb onto his lap and make use of that comfortable couch, then she could really show him what she was made of.

"Azai, Dalissa can help you. Take her to your land. Let her look around and help by being a liaison with the lion pack. This could be what you need to broker a peace treaty for everyone." Gerri walked to the door and opened it. "Dali, while you were exploring, I had your bag delivered. It's right outside for you. Azai, thank you and keep me updated on everything."

Dalissa got up and walked to the door and glanced back at Azai. Gerri was kicking them out? Politely, but still! She heard Azai walk up behind her. He placed his hand against her lower back and the heat traveled straight to her core. She hurried out the door and turned back to look at Gerri. "Thank you for everything. I'll see you soon!"

Dalissa bent to grab her bag and Azai took it from her. "I'm capable of carrying my bag but thank you." Azai set it down and stepped closer. She could feel his breath on her lips.

"I know you can, but why should you when I'm here?"

Dalissa leaned forward and brushed her lips against his. The briefest of touches, but she had to know what his lips felt like. She leaned back and Azai wrapped his arm around her waist, pulling her back to him.

"Temptress," he growled softly. "That wasn't enough for me." He kissed the corner of her mouth, then lightly pressed a kiss to the other side of her mouth before gently pressing his lips against hers.

She moaned and opened her mouth, Azai angled his head, so he could take the kiss deeper. Their tongues dueled and she couldn't tell who moaned, but the sound made her pussy clench in need.

She felt his cock against the juncture of her thighs. Her mind reminded her she hadn't had sex in so long, her pussy had a giant vacancy sign waving him in. Whoa! This was getting too heavy too fast. She hated to do it, but she pulled back from him and groaned at the loss of his lips. Stupid common sense.

"We should go. Anyone could walk out of their apartment and public sex is not on my bucket list." Yeah, right.

The hallway in front of Gerri's apartment was not the best place for sex. In a pinch, she could probably make it work though. What the hell was wrong with her?

She sighed when he let go of her. Was it wrong to want him so much so fast? She turned to walk down the hall. She had to get out of reach of him or they were going to have some serious PDA. And she meant public display of affection. This made her smile. She was thinking about PDA in front of the PDA office. Clearly, lack of sex had made her lose normal brain functions.

"What has you laughing? Did I kiss that badly?"

She glanced over her shoulder at Azai. "Not at all. I was thinking about PDA in front of the PDA." He gave her an odd look and she shook her head. "Never mind."

He walked ahead and looked over his shoulder at her. "Well, either way. I'm available for more anytime you are. Come on, my truck is parked across the street."

Truck? What the hell was that? Not that it mattered. She couldn't wait to see more sights as they drove to his home.

"How far away is your pack and land?" Dalissa wanted it to be a short drive so she could be in the woods that much faster, but she also wanted to sightsee. Not to mention being confined in close quarters with this man who made her body hum and parts she hadn't paid attention to in too long tingle.

She really hadn't expected to find her mate so fast after getting to Earth. He was obviously attracted to her, but what did he think about his mate being from Aurora? Was it too soon to talk about it?

Azai placed her bag in the back of his truck and walked around to open her door. He leaned in close and she felt his body heat behind her. She held herself rigid. If she touched him, she would be all over him. The attraction was crazy and so hard to fight!

"Dalissa, welcome to Earth." Dalissa shivered as he whispered against her ear. "Thank you. I can't wait to see more of it. Thank you, too, for being my guide."

* * *

Dalissa stared at everything in the truck and outside as they passed. The colors were so different than Aurora but just as beautiful. She wasn't sure if it was a quick drive to the pack's land or if she was so focused on the view, she lost track of time, but they had arrived. Trees, grass, cars, and some buildings zoomed by and she was eager to investigate it all.

Azai put the truck in park and turned on the bench seat to look at her. "If you have any trouble with my pack while you're here, come to me right away. We are having issues with the lion pack next door and I don't want that to extend to you."

Dalissa nodded but didn't look at Azai. She watched a man approach the truck and stand in front of it with his hands on his hips. "I think someone is waiting for your attention."

She looked around the area they parked in and saw several houses and lots of trees behind them. It really wasn't that much different than home, except the colors.

NINE

Azai glanced out the windshield of the truck. "Yeah, that's Jed. I think he may have appointed himself a one-man welcoming committee. He's a good guy though. Come on, I'll introduce you."

Azai opened his door and walked around the truck to Dalissa's door. She climbed out and Azai stood close as she brushed against his body. "We aren't done. Next time I kiss you, nothing will stop me." He felt Dalissa shudder, and he leaned back. She was too much temptation.

"You're not the Dali I was expecting to meet, that's for sure." Jed rushed up to stand across from them. "Azai, how did you get that confused?"

Azai growled, hearing the humor in Jed's voice.

"Hi, Jed. I'm Dalissa. Gerri was manipulating the situation as she loves to do and gave me a nickname. I'm growing kind of fond of it actually." Azai watched Dalissa smile and his wolf howled. He wanted that smile turned on him, not his best friend.

"Another interesting fact, you're a lion. Gerri is full of surprises, isn't she? Should I assume by Azai's growl he's your mate?"

Azai wrapped his arm around Dalissa's waist and tugged her against him "I'm going to show Dalissa the house. You can grab her bag and then leave." As they walked away, he heard Jed laughing.

"Do you not want me to answer his question? Are you ashamed a lion is your mate because we don't have to claim each other? We can ignore it and I will spend a few days on Earth and then head back to Aurora." Azai's wolf howled at her words. He was pissed she would even suggest it. But Azai understood why she would say it. He clenched his jaw and guided her into the house.

"Let's make this brief and we can do the full tour later. This is the living room, the kitchen is back there, my office to the right. Up these stairs is my bedroom and two guest rooms." Azai steered her up the stairs and into the first bedroom. He shut the door and locked it. "We need to talk, and you're not leaving my bedroom until we do."

Azai watched as she looked around his room. She wasn't bashful and took everything in carefully. "You can sit on the bed. I won't bite you, yet."

Dalissa smirked over her shoulder at him and walked to the bed. She trailed her hand across the blanket that lay on top. "Let's talk. Are you afraid your pack won't accept a lion, or do you just want to hide me up here and away from everyone?"

Azai watched her hand and imagined it caressing his body. He dragged his eyes away and focused on what she just said. "I'm not ashamed you're a lion. I don't care what you are except mine. You won't leave me, not unless you have a damn good reason. We haven't even tried to see how things go with us. Why would you want to leave?"

"I made an assumption when you hustled me away from Jed." Azai stalked closer to where she stood. "I guess I'm nervous about your pack and how I will be received."

"A mate is not something others get to decide. You're mine and I am yours. They can't change that. I wouldn't let them and whoever made you feel worthless...I will eat them for you."

Dalissa shivered at his words. He wondered if she was imagining him eating her instead. He was thinking about it now and his cock was straining against his jeans.

"I never said anyone made me feel worthless." Dalissa looked into his eyes and trailed off.

"You didn't have to. I can sense it. To your question, Jed was poking fun at me. It was remove him from being so close to you or kill him." Azai leaned in. "Now that we have that cleared up. What are you thinking about a wolf for a mate, and one from Earth at that?"

Dalissa closed her eyes and took a few steps around to the side of the bed "Azai, I... I'm thinking I want my mate to kiss me now."

He stalked toward her, watching her with enough possession to make the hairs on her arms stand on end. He focused on her mouth. She swiped her tongue over her lips, and his eyes darkened, the specks of amber turning brighter by the second.

He stopped in front of her, wrapped his hands around her waist, and hauled her into him. Downstairs, the front door opened.

"Azai, we found another note," Jed hollered. "Remy needs you to come now." Azai groaned and dropped his head onto Dalissa's shoulder. He raised his voice slightly to be heard downstairs. "Give me a minute, Jed, and we will be right there." Azai looked into her eyes. "I need to check this out. Would you like to meet Remy now?"

"Sure, I would like to meet one of Earth's lions and maybe I can help." Azai stepped back and took her hand in his. "You're helping already by being with me. My wolf is calm and so am I."

Azai couldn't help the proud grin that crossed his face as she smiled and walked out the door with him. At the base of the stairs, Jed paced with a frown. Azai expected some kind of joke from him; the letter must be bad.

"Jed, tell me what happened?" Jed glanced up and then down at their joined hands but didn't comment on them. "Mattias was on patrol near where you and Remy meet. He smelled blood and went to investigate." As he talked, he turned and headed outside. "Remy's waiting for us. I'll explain as we walk." He nodded to Dalissa.

Since they hadn't mated, she wouldn't hear them if they shifted, so staying in this form was respectful to her. Azai was pleased his friend was considerate of her.

"On a different tree, he found a perfect circle. It looked as if the bark was cleanly removed and nailed to the tree was a piece of paper." Jed paused and glanced up at the sky. "It was covered in blood."

Just as Jed finished speaking, Dalissa's head jerked up. "I can smell it from here. Can you, Azai?" Azai realized he could, but it was faint, so faint he hadn't noticed it until she said it.

"Didn't you say there was a chemical smell with the first note?" Dalissa looked between her mate and Jed. Azai nodded and sniffed the air. "I don't smell anything besides the blood."

Jed nodded.

"I smell chemicals. It's overshadowed by the blood, but it's there still."

"We're almost there. Did someone send for Remy?" Azai assumed they had but wanted to ask.

As they approached the spot, Remy stepped out of the trees. "Remy, I'm sorry to introduce you this way but this is Dalissa, my mate. Dalissa this is Remy the lion pride king, also known as the Lion King." The guys laughed.

Dalissa looked between the two men.

"Azai, I told you the Lion King jokes get old. Dalissa, a pleasure to you meet you. I welcome you to my pride to meet the local lions anytime." Azai pulled Dalissa closer. His wolf didn't like the unattached males taking to his mate. He was possessive already and it was only getting worse the more time they spent together. "But I have something to give you. This was found on my land, and from what Azai had mentioned earlier, I assumed it is meant for you."

Azai reached out and took the paper Remy held out. Dalissa leaned over his shoulder and read it out loud.

To the woman who entered the apartment building with Gerri Wilder and then later left with a man:

I know what you are. You are not welcome here. Go home.

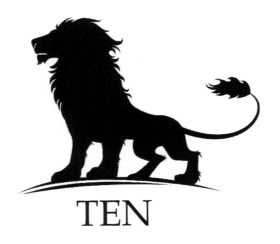

TEN

Dalissa's voice trailed off and she glanced at Remy and then to Jed. Azai's body shook and he growled. "Jed, why don't you and Dalissa take a look at the tree and I will head with Remy to check on this note."

Dalissa was about to protest that she wasn't weak and could be of assistance when she realized he wasn't sending her to his house but to inspect the scrawl on the tree. Finally. Someone realizing she had a brain she could use. And he was her mate. Things only got better and better. Well, aside from the weird notes, but she couldn't get every single thing she wanted.

She hoped it wasn't a big deal, but she was going to let Gerri know so she could watch her apartment just to be safe.

Dalissa turned and walked over to Jed. She glanced over her shoulder to see Azai stalking toward her. When he got close, she turned and wrapped her arms around his neck.

"Go, check out the area with Remy. I'll meet you at the house. Jed will be here to show me around."

Azai growled softly, his voice sending shivers down her spine. Then he kissed her. And her brain cells melted. Her legs went weak and she had to lean into Azai to hold herself up.

"Ahem, can I get Gerri's number please? I would like to get me some of that," Jed said.

Azai quickly let go of her and stepped back. Dalissa tried to keep from laughing when he looked at Jed and glared. It must have dawned on him what he said because Jed quickly backtracked.

"I meant a mate, not Dalissa, dude. The whole forest knows she's yours. Chill."

Dalissa's laughter couldn't be contained any longer. "Come on, Jed. Show me the tree. It's probably smarter if we get you away from Azai right now."

"You got it," Jed nodded. "I agree. He looks ready to tear me limb from limb and I like my limbs."

She turned and followed Jed. "Tell me about your pack. Are the wolves going to accept me as a mate, being a lion?"

Jed laughed and shook his head "If they want to stay in the pack, they will. Azai won't stand for anything less and you wouldn't respect him if he did, right?"

She sighed but gave a slight nod. He was right. A mate should come first always, and it was nice to know Jed saw that in Azai too.

"Tell me about Aurora. I never thought about traveling to another world. Mind you, Azai didn't tell anyone but me and Remy about your home."

"Aurora is very different from your Earth. The colors are the most startling, but our tech is more advanced. Earth is much more populated, that's for sure."

Jed stopped in front of a tree and Dalissa could smell the chemicals. "I can't place what the compounds are, or why they're used, but it's stronger now." Some familiar smells registered in her brain. Earth probably shared some of the fundamental elements of life that were consistent throughout the universe. Each element had its own scent. If she could just pick them out.

Dalissa looked at the note attached to the tree. "*Down the windy path, the lion walks*. Do you think this applies to me or Remy's pride?"

Dalissa peered at the ground around the tree, then walked around trying to identify anything that seemed odd or out of place.

Jed said, "I think this note could be related to the one that was sent to you, but unlikely. I'm not sure if that's good or bad though. What are the chances of two seemingly unrelated issues happening at the same time?"

"I don't know, honestly, but if that person saw me leave Gerri's, then Azai's presence was purely by mistake and coincidental." Dalissa moved in wider circles around the tree. Jed stared at the tree and the perfect circle etched into the bark.

"Jed, come here. Can you smell the chemicals? It seems like it's a trail leading this way." Dalissa shifted into her lion and tracked the smell. She heard Jed behind her. He shifted into his wolf, tearing his clothes and sniffed the ground.

Dalissa followed the scent. It was a straight path, and eventually, they reached a road. She paused and Jed padded up next to her. He waited for a moment, and then moved back to the tree line. Soon after, he was back in his human form, his head poking out from behind a tree.

"Dalissa, I asked one of the wolves to bring

me a change of clothes and get you something. I'll stay back here if you want to look around out there."

She wanted to laugh, but he couldn't hear her anyway. It was sweet he was protecting her privacy. She hadn't even thought about the clothes issue. On her planet, they had technologically advanced clothing that shifted with the animal. So when shifting back, the clothes returned also. Here, shifters destroyed whatever they had on.

She looked back at the ground and trotted forward. In front of her looked to be tire tracks. By the distance between front and back axels, it was a truck or SUV. It was probably a safe bet that whoever left the notes on the tree had walked in from here.

Behind her, she heard Jed talking to someone. A moment later, he stepped out of the trees. "There's some clothes for you to change into." Dalissa trotted behind the tree and shifted then dressed in their clothing to not cause questions to arise. She folded her "clothes" into a small square and shoved it in a pocket.

She headed out to where Jed stood and pointed down the road. "I found tire tracks up there. The smell ended there also. I think the substance was used to destroy the smell of the person. I don't get anything."

Jed rushed over and crouched down to inspect the tracks. "I don't smell anything. I didn't smell the chemical trail you tracked either. Do shifters on Aurora have a stronger sense of smell than we do?"

Dalissa cracked a smile. "Let's head home and I will tell you about shifters on Aurora."

Jed stood. "I'm thinking I like *Dali*. Dalissa is a mouthful. Do you mind if I call you that?"

Did that mean Jed was accepting her into the pack easily? A nickname had to be a good thing!

"I like that. To answer your question, shifters on Aurora are stronger, faster and overall have better senses. Maybe because the shifters on Earth diluted their blood by mating with humans while our lines are full Aurora born shifters. At least, I think that's what happened. I don't know honestly. Never thought about it, but I am glad I could track that scent for you."

* * *

They weren't far from Azai's house, or at least cutting through the woods didn't seem long. Dalissa inspected every tree, piece of grass or stick on the ground. She was fascinated with the animals that lived in the woods surrounded by wolves and lions but didn't seem scared.

"The house is right over there," he pointed

and smiled. "Go in. I'll be out here to talk with Azai when he gets back."

Dalissa glanced where Jed indicated. "Thanks, I'll see you later. It's been an eventful day. I think I will take a bath and lie down until Azai returns."

She headed to the house, glancing around the area as she went. She could feel eyes on her, but no one showed themselves. Then she heard a twig snap. Dali swung around, a bit of fear racing through her. Not far, a woman walked toward her. The female wasn't smiling.

"Who are you?" the stranger asked. "I haven't seen you before."

Dalissa relaxed. She was meeting her first pack member. "Hi," Dalissa said, "I'm Azai's mate. This is my first time here."

"Mate? Really?" the female laughed loudly. "Boy, oh boy. You're going to piss off a lot of people."

Dalissa wasn't thrilled with that comment. She didn't want to cause fighting in the pack. Was this a good idea after all?

The woman offered her hand to shake. "I'm Megan. Part of the lion pack, if you haven't guessed that from my scent. Nice to meet you."

"Nice to meet you too," Dalissa said, not sure if that was true or not.

Megan sniffed then drew her brows down. "I didn't mean to upset you, but that's how it is with an unmated alpha. Pack females always hoping he'd pick them."

Dalissa understood that, but she was here and things were going to change. But change how was the question.

Megan glanced around, nervous. "Look," she said, "I got to be someplace in a few minutes. It was nice to meet you." With that, she headed back the direction she'd come.

Dalissa sighed and stepped into the house. It was weird being in there without Azai. She should wait. Yeah. Exploring the house would be better with Azai's permission.

What if he had some kind of freaky BDSM room and he didn't want her to see it? She snorted, laughing at the idea. Her mind was taking her in all crazy directions. She paused outside Azai's bedroom door and debated going inside. She didn't want to snoop so she went across the hall to a guest bedroom.

She went inside and peered around. Wow. It was gorgeous. Dark wood furniture, full size bed with cream blankets on top. It was warm and inviting. So inviting she decided to skip the bath and take a nap. It had been a long day since she arrived on Earth.

Dali pulled the blanket and top sheet down and slid inside... But her feet got stuck, she couldn't straighten them out. What the hell was wrong with this bed? She climbed out and pulled the blanket off the top and looked at the sheet underneath.

It was folded in half and tucked in, what was the purpose of that? She stared at the bed for a few minutes. She needed to ask about that later, but in the meantime, she remembered she wanted to let Gerri know about the note, so she pulled her communicator out and called Gerri. Hopefully, she would be close to her office and be able to answer.

A moment later, an image of Gerri popped up. "Is everything okay, Dalissa? I expected you to not need me for a while, if at all. And to use the communicator rather than Azai's cell..." Gerri frowned. "What's wrong?"

"I'm sorry, Gerri. Everything's fine here. Azai had to check on something and I didn't know about a cell. I'm calling to let you know a note was delivered to the lion pride for me. Yeah, for me," she said, just as surprised as Gerri seemed. "It said for me to go home. That I wasn't wanted here. I'm safe here on pack land, so I'm not worried. Anyways, I wanted you to know someone was watching your place."

Gerri nodded and her blue eyes flashed with

her animal. "Let me know if Azai needs backup. Don't worry about me. I can take care of myself, but just in case, I'll make sure I have some help here. Thank you, dear, for letting me know."

Dalissa hung up the com and fell back on top of the bed, lost in thought. It didn't take long for her to drift off to sleep.

ELEVEN

Azai walked into his house and followed the delicious scent of his mate to the guest room. He knocked lightly and opened the door. He paused when he saw her spread out on top of the sheet and the blanket on the floor. It dawned on him what happened. Ah, fuck. He forgot to fix the sheet. She wasn't supposed to sleep in there.

He quietly headed over to the bed and crawled across the mattress until he was lying next to her. "Dalissa, love. Wake up."

She groaned and stretched her body, her sexy brown eyes blinking awake. "Hi," she said in that husky voice that drove him to distraction. "When did you get back?"

He glanced at her shirt stretched tightly

across her chest "Those aren't the clothes you were wearing earlier. Did something happen?"

Dalissa laughed and he loved the wide grin on her face. "No, I shifted tracking the chemical smell earlier. Jed had clothes brought to me. Maybe I should take them off so I can give them back."

Azai groaned as he watched her climb off the bed. She lifted the shirt and tossed it behind her. She wasn't wearing a bra and his wolf itched to get out and mate her. Then she unsnapped her jeans and he couldn't take his eyes off her hands. He scooted off the bed and grabbed her around the waist. Pulling her to him, she straddled his waist and sniffed at his neck and flicked her tongue over his throat. Azai moaned when he felt her tongue across his skin.

She lifted her face to his, and their mouths met in a frantic mating. He didn't as much kiss as he possessed. He conquered her with his tongue, rubbing the inside of her mouth with enough passion, he thought he'd burst into flames.

The world shifted, and he scooped her into his arms. They needed to go to his room. As he turned around, she kissed his throat, licking at the pulse beating erratically. She grazed her teeth over his neck and nipped at his warm flesh. Ah, shit. Fuck waiting. He groaned and dropped her on the bed.

"Tell me now if you don't want this." He gave her a heated look.

She got on her knees on the bed. Lust shot through him. He clenched his jaw. She grabbed the zipper of her jeans and started to pull them down.

"Stop." The growl was almost unintelligible.

"Tell me." He growled out at her. "I need to hear you say the words."

"I want you, Azai. Now. Right now."

Flames licked at his skin.

She panted while he ripped off his clothes in hurried movements. The sound of tearing cloth enhanced his arousal, thickening the blood in his veins. He stood next to the bed with his cock standing proud, pointing to his belly button.

Pre-cum oozed from his slit, sliding down the sides of his long length. Passion overran every other thought in his brain. He needed her. Their lips met in a desperate kiss, and she whimpered. She splayed her hands over his chest.

"You're so strong," she murmured. "I can feel how hard it is for you to control your animal."

He groaned, loving her soft, husky tone. "It's damn near killing me."

He cupped her breasts and squeezed the aching mounds. Rolling the twin tips between his fingers, he brought her to the edge. He nibbled her neck, her lips, and traveled down until he latched on to a nipple.

She moaned. He slid his hands down her body while flicking his tongue over one swollen nipple. Everywhere his hands touched felt like silk. He detached from her nipple and pushed her to lie back on the pillows on the bed.

He sat on his heels, watching her. *Mine. Mine. Mine.* Yes. She fucking was his and he was going to take her now. His mate. His woman. She lay there, completely naked and spread eagle, his gaze devoured her body.

"So beautiful. I'm going to eat you up until all your honey drips on my tongue. Then I'm going to make you come--and you will come--on my tongue. Your sweet honey's going to slide down my throat and fill me with your scent," he said.

Azai watched as she bunched the sheets in her fists. He kissed her foot. Harsh moans came from her lips. He licked, kissed, and nibbled up her ankle, to her knee, up her thigh until he stopped a hairsbreadth from her pussy. She gasped for air. He loved seeing how difficult the simple task of breathing was for her as he touched her. He wanted to draw out the tension, watch her squirm until she begged.

He lowered onto his belly and flashed

golden eyes at her. Arousal had tightened his features into rigid lines and severe angles. He pushed her legs apart, making room for his large, bulky shoulders, and wrapped his arms around her thighs. His hot breath stroked her heated folds. Her body jerked off the bed when he buried his nose into her sex.

"Mine," he growled into her pussy. The vibration from his lips made her shudder and moan.

"Oh god," she cried and rocked her hips over his lips.

He licked a slow trail around her entrance and up her clit. He noticed each swipe ratcheted up her panting. He licked at her cream as if it were the tastiest dessert in the world. He watched her eyes as he feasted between her thighs.

She groaned and moaned. It was music to his ears. As she tossed her head side to side, he felt her body tense. She was close. He slipped his tongue into her slick channel and fucked her with quick, merciless swipes.

"Azai! God, you're killing me."

He moved his tongue faster. Harder.

"Yes, yes, yes!" She whimpered, squeezing the blankets in a white-knuckle grip. Azai growled, his possessive wolf loved seeing her lose control.

He knew she'd fall off the edge at any moment. He sucked on her swollen clit hard and she screamed. Her whole body shook as she came. In a wave of shudders, her climax coated his lips. She gasped, her legs shaking at the sides of his head. He slid his hot body up hers, stopping when the head of his cock kissed her swollen sex.

Their eyes met and she smiled, her eyes bright and full of desire. "I need you."

She twined her hands into his hair and pulled him down. They kissed, almost devouring each other with the depth of their lust. She curled her legs around his muscled ass and whimpered. The hard length of his shaft lay between her legs, slipping and sliding over her wet pussy lips. He wanted his cock inside and he didn't want to wait any longer.

A soft purr left her lips and made his own animal yank at the inner chains. Fuck! That had to be the sexiest sound ever.

He pulled his hips back and slid his length into her completely. Her pussy fluttered, grasping at his driving shaft. Fuck, she felt absolutely perfect.

"Oh my god," she whispered. "That's...amazing."

"You're so tight. God, you feel good, but just hold on a second," he said through gritted teeth.

Something wild and untamed inside him took hold. She dug her nails into his shoulders and wiggled her hips under him. She kissed his neck, grazing her teeth over his pounding pulse, and bit his shoulder. Her nails raked down his back, biting painfully into his skin.

She continued to bite him, and he groaned. Holding the savage side of him back was costing him. It wasn't going to last much longer and he knew any second now, he'd lose all control. "I-I can't hold back..."

"Then don't. Just...fuck me...already."

He lost it. Lost all control. All sense of holding back. It was all about taking her. Owning her. Stamping his scent inside her. Making it so it was only him and his cock she'd ever think of.

He slammed into her in repeatedly. She whimpered with every drive of his cock into her. Over and over, he thrust and pulled back. She panted and clung to him, her nails scraping down his arms. He groaned, and she moaned with every slap of skin on skin.

"Yes. Just like that. Hard, fast. I love it." Pleasure blasted through him and traveled through his blood in a fiery rush. Every pant, every moan, every time her nails dragged trails on his skin, let him know she was his.

His moves became wilder, his thrusts

harsher, faster. With every slide of his cock into her, he saw stars.

"Damn..." His voice sounded strained.

She lifted off the pillows onto her elbows. She swiped her tongue over his shoulder and licked his salty flesh. Her tongue against his skin made him thrust harder, she dropped back onto the bed, throwing her head side to side. He slipped a hand between their slick bodies and rubbed a finger on her clit.

She choked out his name as her body shook under him. He slowed his thrusts and tensed above her. God, yes. Her pussy tightened around his cock, driving him to his own release. He dropped his head into her shoulder, growled, and licked at her galloping pulse. His cock jerked inside her, spreading warmth into her and filling her womb with his seed.

He landed on the bed beside her and quickly moved her to lie in his arms next to him. "I'm sorry about the sheets, I'll explain tomorrow, but for now, sleep, my love."

TWELVE

The next morning, Dalissa woke early and opened her eyes to see Azai staring at her. "How long have you been awake and why are you staring at me?"

"Good morning, love. I just woke and saw you starting to stir." Azai leaned down and kissed her lightly. Dalissa was afraid to open her mouth and give him a deep kiss. Morning breath could wipe a relationship out fast. She had a hard time believing the humans on Aurora who said their mates never had morning breath. Shifters from her planet couldn't be that perfect.

"Are you hungry? Meet me downstairs in thirty minutes. I'll cook breakfast." Azai nuzzled his nose into her neck and climbed out of bed.

"There's a shower through there. I brought your bag up last night."

She watched him walk out and smiled at the ceiling. She was giddy like a little child with a new toy, but he was perfect and so much better than she expected to find. She reluctantly climbed out of bed and went into the shower, memories of last night accompanied her and she turned the shower to cold water. If she was getting off, it would be with him, not by herself.

A few minutes later, she was dried off and opening her bag. Across the room on the floor, she spotted his shirt and decided that was more comfortable for breakfast and easy access for a quickie if they had time. She grinned. Here she was planning a quickie after a whole night of crazy, dirty sex. That vacancy sign in her vagina had been tossed in the trash. But she had a feeling Jed was the type to show up unannounced.

She wandered down the stairs and smelled coffee and bacon cooking. Oh, man. Coffee. Bacon. She'd heard amazing things about both and when Zaria had some brought to Aurora, she'd been the first to try them. She'd fallen in total lust ever since.

He was the perfect man. He gave her orgasms in bed and caffeine and bacon afterward. He couldn't be real. Gerri deserved the biggest fucking sexbot for this. Then again, maybe a fruit basket or a case of Sidaii was a better idea. She had a feeling Gerri wasn't lacking in the sex department.

"You're amazing," she murmured and moaned at the delicious scents of food and her man. She rushed across the kitchen and hugged Azai from behind, rubbing her cheek against his back.

"Ah, babe," he groaned, the scent of his desire filling the area. "Are you marking me like a cat? It's okay but forewarn a guy."

She smacked his ass and pulled herself up to sit on the counter next to him.

"We need to work on your cat and lion jokes, wolfman. I'm sure between Remy and me, we can come up with a few that fit you wolves. By the way, what was up with my sheets?"

His face turned crimson and the scent of his embarrassment made her scrunch her nose. "Are you blushing?"

She bounced a little on the countertop. She couldn't wait to hear what he had to say.

He cleared his throat. "About that. When I thought Dali, a guy, was showing up. Well, Jed and I wanted to have some fun and see what kind of sense of humor he had. When I realized Dali was you and my mate, I didn't think to tell you not to sleep in there. You were going to be in my bed every night anyway."

She shook her head. "Cocky bastard."

Azai yanked up an eyebrow at her and she laughed. It went without saying. She had never met an alpha male who wasn't a bit cocky. Then again most alpha females were too.

"I think you need a spanking for calling me names. Should I bend you over my knee now?" Oh, damn. So maybe he did have a kinky room full of toys. That idea held so much promise. She squirmed and Azai stepped between her legs. "That excites you, doesn't it?"

She reached over and shut the burner off and moved the bacon to another unlit burner. "If it does, what are you going to do about it?"

Azai grinned, and lust flooded her system, short-circuiting her brain cells in the process. He grabbed the hem of her shirt and pulled it over her head. He tossed it aside and bent down and fluttered kisses over her chest and sucked a nipple into his mouth. Molten lava spread through her. She rubbed her hands over his muscled chest. He was solid. Strong. Hers. All hers. The thought made her hotter. She slid a hand down his body, dipped into his boxers, and wrapped it around his cock.

He was hard, hot, and smooth. She pumped his length in a slow glide. He growled, and she smiled.

She brushed the pad of her thumb over his nipple and pinched the tight little bud.

He sucked on one of her breasts, then the other, and back until she was ready to beg him to fuck her.

"If I don't have you soon, I may lose the little sanity I have left. I need you." His sexy rumble turned up the heat inside her.

"Then have me. I'm all yours."

His growl added to the desperation riding her. He tore off his boxers in the time it took her to let out a soft moan. When he pulled her to the edge of the counter, she thought she'd fall, but he slid her over his cock and slipped inside her in one smooth glide.

She twined her legs and arms around his waist and neck. She ended up wrapped tightly around him. Arousal surrounded them like a thick blanket. She smashed her lips to his and moaned into the eager union. He turned, and her back hit the smooth surface of the fridge.

He fucked her mouth with his tongue, mimicking the movements he made with his cock.

The fridge moved with each of his thrusts. The contents of the fridge crashed into each other, making large breaking noises.

Heat spread inside her. He squeezed her ass. The combination of actions made her pussy flutter in seconds. His fast, pummeling drives pushed her to dig her nails into his shoulders. She wrenched her lips from his and moaned louder. Electricity buzzed in her veins, building up the need for more.

"Oh god. Oh yes. Yes, yes, yes." Tight pressure rippled inside her body. Muscles she'd never used before became stiff as she closed the distance to ecstasy. She snapped. A scream lodged in her throat as she came. Pleasure flared brightly, overflowing and rushing through her.

Mine.

Mine.

Mine.

He continued to thrust in and out of her. His nibbles on her jaw and shoulder pushed her orgasm to go on and on. Seconds later, he shuddered. He snarled a curse into her neck and made her body vibrate with the force of his release. Semen shot into her channel and bathed her womb with his cum. Fuck, yes. It was perfect. Oh, so perfect to be filled by him in every sense.

They were catching their breaths and staring at each other, his cock still pulsing inside her for long moments.

He kissed her softly, his tongue gliding over

her bottom lip. "This time we can shower together, then breakfast, and I mean real food, next time."

She giggled at his words and wrapped her legs around his waist. He held her by her bare ass and carried her up the stairs.

* * *

Two hours later they were sitting fully dressed at the kitchen table enjoying cold bacon and hot coffee.

There was a knock at the door, and it opened soon after. It was Jed.

He grinned at them, wagging his brows. "I should probably have waited to be invited in, from the sounds I heard when I dropped by this morning. Seeing anything tied to that could cause permanent blindness."

Azai growled at him, no one was seeing his mate but him. "Jed, watch it. If you accidentally ever see my mate naked, I will skin you alive. Don't ever forget that."

Dalissa snorted and got up to grab the coffee pot. "Jed, would you like a cup of coffee?" She glanced over her shoulder and grabbed a cup when he nodded.

Azai watched her walk to the table and set

the mug in front of Jed, then she came over and sat on his lap. "Would you like more coffee, love?"

Azai's chest puffed out with pride. She chose to sit with him. His woman was beautiful and perfect. He loved how sweet and naturally humble she was. No pretentions, just her. It was hard to know the real female nowadays. Most of them hid behind whatever it was they wanted men to see. Not Dali. She was too innocent. Pure of heart.

"Thanks, Dali. Coffee is exactly what I wanted this morning," Jed said with a sigh. "This is good."

Azai growled again. He had to get his wolf under control. He didn't like anyone familiar with his mate. When they were officially mated, he might relax. He was pleased Jed kept the nickname and treated her like a friend already. That was good. He wanted Dali to feel welcomed into the pack and not worry about staying on Earth with a pack of wolves.

"Tell me what you found last night, and I'll tell you what we found." Azai was anxious to hear but he didn't want to tell Dalissa what he found. He wanted her far away from the area. He didn't care if she was a lioness. He wanted to protect her.

THIRTEEN

Dalissa really wanted to hear what they found out about the note that was sent to her. It was just a note and nothing had been done. Yet. Her mind was messing with her, constantly thinking someone was watching. Technically, no crime had been committed, but for someone to leave a note on land surrounded by shifters...It wasn't good no matter how you looked at it.

How did they get on the land or did that mean there was someone in one of the groups doing this? Was it a pride member hating the pack or vice versa?

"Azai, have you thought that someone in your pack or Remy's pride was doing this? It would make sense a shifter could get onto the land and no one else notice."

Azai frowned. "Tell me what you found first, and we can discuss that idea next."

She sipped on her coffee and thought back. "When we approached the tree, I smelled the compounds stronger than before. I circled the perimeter of the tree until I caught the trail of the chemical leading away. Jed and I shifted and followed the trail to the road where we found tire tracks. And the smell ended there. I think the compounds covered the scent trail. Could be anybody."

Jed smiled at her with pride. "Azai, I couldn't smell the trail at all. Your mate is something else. She has one hell of a sniffer."

Dalissa felt his arms around her waist tighten a little.

"If it were someone in our pack or Remy's pride, they wouldn't have to drive to the land and walk in. So, my guess is a shifter, but one that neither group marks as an outsider for some reason."

Dalissa thought about that for a few minutes.

"You said the lion pride is new to the area, so any scent outside your wolves would be assumed as theirs and they would assume the same of yours, right?"

Jed had a shocked look on his face, whether

from her idea or that it came from her she wasn't sure. "Shit, that's a good point. Don't you think, Azai?"

Azai nodded, his face grim. "It makes sense why someone would drive up but neither pack noticed. Jed, put patrols on the road in that area."

"On it right now, alpha boss." He took a long swig of coffee and placed the mug on the table. "Thanks for the coffee, Dali," he smiled at her and then turned to Azai. "I'll get back to you if anything else happens."

Once Jed was gone, Dalissa got on her feet, turned and straddled Azai's lap.

"Now tell me what you found out about my note, please." She curled her arms around his neck, wiggling her hips and rubbing her pussy against his cock. He was staring at her like she was a piece of cake and he had a sweet addiction. His cock strained against his zipper, making her wiggling heat her blood in record time.

"You're killing me," he groaned. "Stay still or I'll turn you over my knee. This time it won't be just a threat."

She debated squirming around or sitting still, the temptation to see how far he would take it was almost worth it. First, though, she had to know what he found out.

"I will be good...for now. Spill." She leaned

into his chest so her breasts pressed at his pecs and didn't move a muscle.

Azai groaned then sighed. "You're going to be the death of me. The kid who took the note didn't pay any attention to who gave it to him. He said it was a man who paid him fifty bucks to deliver it to the woman who arrived in the truck this afternoon. He said the man described Azai's truck, so that was how Remy knew to bring it to me. The only thing we found was a scent. Neither of us had smelled it before."

Dalissa was shocked. How could they not have smelled it before? It seemed to scare Azai. "Okay, why do you look so nervous?"

He sighed and laid his head on her chest. For a moment, he didn't say anything, just rested. When he lifted his head, he wouldn't look her in the eye.

"I think you should go back to Aurora for a little while."

She jumped to her feet, slapped her hands to her hips and glared down at him.

"What? Why would you send me away?" She didn't even bother hiding her anger at him. "I'm stronger than Earth shifters, faster too. I don't need you to protect me! I'm not scared of a human. I'm not scared of anyone. I don't get it..." she sucked in a harsh breath. "You think I'm weak."

Azai stood and rushed forward, but stopped a few steps shy from where she stood. "No. No, Dali. I don't—"

She put a hand up to stop him from talking. She fought back tears. "I need time alone. I don't want to see you until I come back." If she came back.

Dalissa let the door slam behind her. She stalked away, not having a clue where she was going, nor caring at this point. Her mate had no faith or trust in her. How could she live with someone like that? She couldn't. Her parents already proved that.

She pulled out her com unit and dialed Gerri. "You've got to talk some sense into that man," Dali said.

"What's he done now?" Gerri asked.

"He told me I should go back to Aurora because I am too weak." Tears burst out. "I'm a failure, Gerri. My own mate doesn't believe in me." She wiped water blurring her vision.

"Is this all from that letter?" Dalissa nodded. The 3D image focused on her. Gerri sighed. "Let me talk to him. You have to remember he's a male alpha, but that's no excuse. Where are you?"

Dali looked around and noticed she was close to the trees where the acid was used. "I can't go back, Gerri. I can't live like that any longer." She disconnected and felt eyes on her again. Every time she was out, it seemed, someone was watching her.

"Dalissa? Is that you?" Megan's voice came from a short distance.

Dali wiped at her eyes with her shirt. "Yeah, Megan. Sorry." Her new friend came into sight.

"What's wrong?" Megan gave her a big hug. "Did something happen?"

She sucked in a heaving breath, deciding what she wanted to tell her. "Can you give me a ride?" Dali asked.

"Sure, sweetie. My car isn't too far." Megan took her hand and led her through the woods. "Where do you want to go?"

"To a power plant."

FOURTEEN

After his mate stormed out, Azai paced the house, wondering what to do. This mate thing was entirely new. He could really use advice from his dad, but he and his mother were on vacation in the mountains in Europe. No telling if they had cell service there or not. Not to mention the time difference.

Shit. His wolf was tearing at him to get out. Go find her and bring her back. He wanted to agree, but was that the right thing to do? Did he let her cool down first? Should he let her rant and rave at him then tell her she was going back anyway? Should he give her flowers? She'd probably throw them at him.

When his cell phone rang, he knocked over

the sofa to get to it. She was calling back to apologize and agree with him. When he saw Gerri's name on the ID, he frowned.

He picked it up. "Gerri," he said, "you've got to talk some sense into her."

"Into her?" Gerri replied. "Sure it isn't the other way around?"

"What do you mean?" He was clueless.

"Azai," she said, "sit down. I have some news for you."

Worried, he fell into a chair at the kitchen table. "What? Is Dali hurt?"

"Yes, Azai. She is very hurt. You have no faith in her. She's crushed. How could you not believe in your mate?"

"I believe in her, Gerri. It's just. . .she's my mate. I can't have her in danger."

He heard a sigh. "Azai, have you forgotten you're the alpha of the pack?"

"No," he answered. "What's that got to do with anything?" He wasn't sure, but he thought she might've growled *stupid men*.

"It has everything to do with it. Dalissa is your true mate, yes?"

"Yeah." That was the only type of mate he would accept. Otherwise, he would've chosen a female from the pack.

"When was the last time you heard of an alpha male whose true mate wasn't as alpha as he was?"

"Never, I don't think," he answered.

"Exactly," she said.

He still didn't get it.

Gerri sighed again. "Azai, if I didn't know you so well, I'd kick your ass for being so alpha. Listen to me. Dalissa is your alpha mate. That means she's stronger, bigger, faster than others. She can hold her own against anyone but a male alpha. And being from Aurora, I'd wager she'd kick your ass too."

"But, Gerri—"

"No, Azai. There are no excuses. If you can't have faith in her to lead with you, then I'm taking her back home."

His wolf roared and jumped at his skin. The phone fell from his half-shifted hand and anger tore through him. No one would take his mate from him. He heard Gerri's voice coming from the floor.

"That's what I thought," she said. "Your wolf trusts and believes in her. It knows. You're the only one with his head up his ass. If she was meant to be with you, then she has the ability needed to survive as an alpha. Trust her."

He so wanted to disagree, but maybe the woman had a point. Mother Nature knew what she was doing. He picked up the phone.

"Azai, tell her what you're feeling. Tell her why you wanted, past tense, her to leave. If she sees it's because you care for her, then maybe she'll understand and let you keep some of your ass."

"Yeah, okay." He could at least let things ride for a day or two to see how she handled everything. He'd watch over her like a hawk. "Where is she? I'll talk to her."

"Let me take care of getting her. You stay there and think of ways to grovel."

* * *

After telling Megan where the power plant was, Dalissa took the tissue from her and dabbed at her nose. "Thank you for stopping what you were doing to help me."

"Not a problem," she replied. "Anything for a lioness."

Dali smiled back but wasn't sure how to take that reply. If she wasn't a lion, would that mean she wouldn't have helped? Of course not. Her anger at Azai was spreading into all her thoughts.

Dali asked, "Why isn't your car with the others at the pride?"

"I live outside the group. So I drive to come over."

"Why? Don't you miss the community?"

Megan grunted. "I get enough of that with no problem. I have issues with stupid lions, and our pack seems full of them. Mostly males."

So was this woman a specie-ist and a man hater? What would she think if she knew Dali was from another planet? Couldn't be good.

"Besides," Megan continued, "I don't have to worry about others dropping by unexpectedly all the time. That drove me nuts. Remy was the worst."

Dali laughed. "Jed has a tendency to visit at the worst times."

"Exactly." Megan glanced at her. "Anything you want to talk about?"

Dali sighed. "I don't know if you want to hear about my pathetic life."

"Nonsense," Megan said. "Your life isn't pathetic. It's the wolf that's making it so problematic for you."

Dali looked at her. "You think so?"

"Of course. Lion shifters are the top of the

food chain. All the others are jealous of our position and want to bring us down."

That surprised her. "So you think the pride shouldn't have moved so close to the wolf pack? That the wolves are bad news?" Could this woman be the culprit for the tree writings? The tracks were of a truck, not a car. Nix that thought.

"No," Megan said, "just the opposite. Being close is pretty ideal to me. I'm liking it."

Well, never mind that idea.

"So tell me about yourself," Megan asked. "What makes you so much better?"

"Better?" Dali said. "I don't think I'm better."

"You smelled the chemical none of the others did, right?"

Dali remembered Jed telling Azai about her ability to smell what he couldn't. He seemed so proud. She shrugged. She couldn't tell the lion shifter that she was from a different planet. That had to remain a secret.

"I guess I'm just more sensitive or something," she answered.

Megan laughed and patted her hand. "Don't worry, girlfriend. It's okay to admit we're superior. Plus, women are smarter. Men can only fight and kill. We bring life into the world. Being humble is a good thing."

Ah, Dalissa understood now. Megan was one of those who were down on men. Her friend didn't seem like a man hater, but who knew?

Dalissa asked, "Do you have a mate?"

Megan scowled. "No. He was killed when an enemy pride attacked."

She waited for the woman to continue, but she didn't. Instead, the woman glanced in the rearview mirror and frowned.

"What," Dali asked.

"It's probably nothing," her friend said, "but the same car has been behind us since we left."

Dalissa twisted in the seat to look out the back window. All she could tell was the car was dark colored and not a truck. So it wasn't Azai. Her heart crushed a little.

"What's at this power plant where you're going?" Megan asked.

Dali couldn't lie; the shifter would smell it. But she couldn't give her the truth either. "It's a shortcut to my home." Megan glanced at her waiting for more, but she couldn't come up with a partially true cover story. Her mind didn't work that way.

"Oh, good," Megan said. "The car turned off. No stalker, I guess." Dalissa snapped her head around to her friend. Megan laughed. "What? I was joking, sweetie."

"Sorry. I'm uptight." She didn't want to tell the lioness about the creeper-jeepers she'd felt since arriving nor about the letter telling her to go home. Whoever sent the note should be happy — at least one person was.

Megan slowed and turned onto the drive to the parking lot. "Where do you want me to drop you off?"

That was a good question. She barely remembered where she and Gerri got into the car when they left. She was even less sure how to get to the portal.

Dalissa pointed to a side road. "Turn here." When they drove forward, she recognized the area. "This is it."

Megan rolled to a stop. "Are you sure about this?" A couple men in blue jumpsuits walked by, wearing hard hats.

No. "Yes." Sorta.

Megan reached into the back seat and pulled her purse forward. "I'm coming with you."

FIFTEEN

"What?" Dali said, panic rising. "No, you can't." Megan raised a brow at her. "I mean, you don't need to do that. I appreciate it, but I'll be fine."

Megan punched the door locks. "I will not let you roam around with strange men. Even though you are a lioness and can handle yourself, I don't trust a lot of men and one shifter. You can only do so much when outnumbered. Believe me. I know."

Dalissa looked at her new friend. The woman thought she wasn't weak, that she could take care of herself. Why didn't her mate see the same thing?

She recalled that she and Gerri came up from

the portal via a metal box. If she could find that, then she could tell Megan she was fine the rest of the way.

She squeezed Megan's hand. "You are a great friend. Let's go." Both climbed from the car and she searched for the door. There were two and she wasn't sure which one. Only one way to choose: eeny meeny miney mo. The left door it was. Dali set off with Megan on her heels.

Dali pulled open the door and stepped into the dim area. The lobby was familiar with its checkered tile floor and a large window looking over the main floor. Through the window, Dalissa glimpsed the giant blue turbines and large pipes running into an abyss. She'd been so excited when she'd arrived that she didn't remember if they passed this or not.

She opened another door to a dark hall. This could've been right. "You sure about this, Dalissa?" Megan sounded like she'd changed her mind about escorting her.

Dali sighed. "See, there's no one here for the most part. The workers are on the floor and other areas. Besides, I worry about you getting lost on the way back. So, let's get you to your car so you can get home to the pride."

Megan's concerned eyes studied her. "Are you sure?"

"Absolutely." Megan took her hand and guided her into the sunlight, then to her car. "Tell Remy I said bye."

"I will. Anything for the alpha wolf?"

Was there anything to tell him? "No, there's nothing left to say."

Her friend nodded and turned the car around. The lioness waved as she pulled out of the parking lot. Dali let out a huge breath. "Thank god. That could've been difficult."

Instead of going through the same door, Dali went to the other. The lobby was identical to the other one. That was no help. She passed through a doorway into the dim hall. She lifted her nose to see if a scent existed. Gerri's perfume tickled her nose. Yes! She turned a corner following the trail.

Somewhere in the near distance, a door closed. In fact, she'd bet it was the door she came in. "Megan?" She jogged back to the first hall and glanced toward the closed door to the lobby. She waited. When no one came through, she went back to the pathway home. She passed many more doors, wondering where they went. Probably offices and other rooms.

Behind her, footsteps echoed off the concrete floor. Or were they in front of her? She couldn't tell. Was this the same person who entered the lobby? "Hello?" Then as quickly as they appeared, they stopped. "Is someone here?" Only the hum of the air conditioning blowing through the narrow passageway answered her.

Shit. Now she was creeped out big time. She continued forward and the steps restarted. Shit, shit, shit. She tried the knob of the next door she came to. Locked. Same for the next and next. The steps were getting closer.

She came to an intersection and turned, not caring if it was the correct way or not. The echoes ran to catch up with her. Wouldn't matter if the next door was locked or not; she was going through it. A metal break in the wall looked hopeful. She pushed through a door marked *employees only* to a catwalk around the top of a warehouse with pipes running *everywhere*. She had to find somewhere to hide until she was sure this person stalking her, really wasn't.

A stair going down led to another level. She skipped two steps at a time, then ducked behind pipes coming through the floor. To her horror, the footsteps entered. They passed overhead and continued around. A man in a suit and hard hat paused at another door, pulled something from his slacks' pocket then walked out.

Dalissa slid to the floor, back against the pipe, her lungs sucking in air, pulse pounding in her ears. What the fuck was wrong with her? It was the middle of the morning where probably hundreds of employees worked. Gerri did say the workers were puzzled about her coming and going.

When had she become paranoid? The minute she stepped out of the building with Gerri. Stupid. She climbed back to her feet and the stairs. Maybe Azai and her parents were right. She was too weak to be on Earth. Hearing innocent footsteps, the first thing through her mind was a stalker.

Reaching the thick metal door, she leaned against it but it didn't move. What the fuck? She pushed harder, but not even a budge. Had that man locked it? No freaking way! Every other door had been locked, why not this one too? Shit. What were the chances the door the guy left through was locked?

With no options, she walked around and tested her chances. They really sucked. Of course, the door was locked.

"Dalissa?" She spun around, hearing her name.

"Gerri!" she hollered to the woman holding the metal door open. "Don't close the door." Dalissa hurried around and hugged the petite matchmaker. "I'm so glad you're here." She pulled back when Gerri laughed. "What are you doing here?" Dalissa asked.

"A lucky guess on my part," Gerri said. "Since you weren't at my apartment, I didn't know where else you'd go. Good thing my sniffer caught your scent. I would've walked right on by this door." Dalissa hugged her again. "Okay, okay. Let's get to the car. I talked with Azai."

SIXTEEN

After Dalissa's chat with Gerri on the way to the pack, she was willing to give her mate another chance. But if his mind didn't change, she'd have Gerri take her right back to the portal.

Standing in the front room of his cabin, he snarled and sighed. "You being weak never crossed my mind. I swear. I only said it because you're my mate. I want you safe. I don't want you to be in any danger." He took another step closer. "Honestly, some humans are scary as hell. Some fear us because we have animals inside, but humans are so much more savage than we ever could be."

She refused to let that change things. "If we are to be mated, have any kind of relationship, there has to be trust. That means you trust me to take care of myself. I know you have my back and will always try to keep me safe. I get that. I'm ready to do the same for you."

She stared at him, hoping he'd see her point of view. "This won't be the only time there might be some type of danger. You can't just bundle me away and send me to Aurora or anywhere to keep me from danger like I'm a cub. I know how to handle myself. You have to believe in me. My lioness would kill to stay close to you. Don't make me fight her and you."

"You don't understand. I'd die if something happened to you," he said, his voice soft and worried.

Dalissa stepped forward that brought them flush against each other. "I know. I would too if it were you. But we're a team. That's what mates are, Azai. A team. We can face anything together. Anything."

He sighed and wrapped his arms around her waist. "All right. You win." He placed a kiss on her lips and raised his hands to cup her face. "You're not from here, so do me a huge favor and be extra vigilant. Watch your back. I need you. I can't and won't lose you now that I found you."

"Hey, Azai!" Jed yelled from outside.

He growled and she grinned.

"Can you come out front?" Jed asked. "There's something you need to see."

Azai groaned. "What does Jed want now?"

Dalissa held Azai's hand as they headed to the front door where Jed stood waiting. Tears ran down Jed's face and panic bloomed in her chest. She glanced at Azai behind her. Jed didn't look hurt or even sad, so she didn't understand why the tears. In fact, he was laughing. It was then she realized what the phrase laughing until crying meant.

She pushed open the screen door and walked out onto the deck. Standing in front of Azai's house was a line of women. She could smell they were all wolves.

"Azai, are they here because they're upset I'm a lion and your mate?" She couldn't figure out what was going on until Azai groaned and Jed sat down on the step laughing harder. To her right, she saw a group of women led by Remy coming from the woods.

"Fuck!" Azai growled. "I forgot. Dammit, Jed!" He glared at his friend. "You could have reminded me." He shook his head in confusion. "Why would Remy go through with it? He knows she's my mate and not what we thought."

Dalissa began to put some of the pieces together. By the women lined up and the mention of Dali. Oh, boy. Someone had messed up big time. This was obviously some prank he had set up for the person they thought was coming.

Azai gave her a pained look. "I'm not sure how to explain this..."

Remy said, "Tell your woman you planned an epic prank and forgot to cancel it when you realized she wasn't a *he*." He slapped a hand on Jed's arm and grinned wide. "We, being good friends, let it happen because we wanted you to squirm." Remy barely finished talking before bursting into laughter.

Dalissa turned to Azai, a smile on her lips and shaking her head. "You're a devious man. I think two pranks on me mean I get at least one back. Beware, dear." Dalissa turned and looked at everyone gathered. What better moment than to grab the bull by the horns.

"Hi, everyone," she cleared her throat and smiled at the mass of women. That was a lot of females. She hoped nobody held a grudge. The last thing she wanted was more drama. "Since you're here I might as well introduce myself and ask for your help. My name is Dalissa and I am the true mate to the Alpha of the White Tip Pack. I am also a lioness." There was a loud gasp. "Yes. A lioness, but that's not what I need your help with. Not much I can do about the jungle fever going on in this relationship."

Everyone laughed and her nerves calmed.

"Here's my dilemma. If the men of your pack or pride are like Azai, they don't want you in on the action, right?" A murmur of assent and head nods greeted her. She sighed. "Talking about protecting you like you're children, huh?"

"Damn straight," said an older woman from the lion side, her features looked like she was permanently annoyed. "Like they forget how strong women are."

Behind her, she heard Jed, Remy, and Azai whispering to each other.

Dalissa nodded. "Exactly my point. You see, I was delivered a note from a human. Not a very nice note either."

The women standing in front of her turned and whispered to each other for a moment. From the group of lionesses, the same woman who'd spoken up before stepped forward. "My name is Old Bertha. I'm tired of standing here. What do you want us to do? We aren't hiding from any danger."

Remy coughed and apologized quietly behind Dalissa. "It's the southern way. We parade our crazy out front and Bertha is as southern as you get. She's got a good heart though."

Dalissa tried not to laugh. What in the world had she gotten herself into? Oh, well. At least they weren't discriminating against her.

"The human delivered a message to a lion to pass to us. What I need is for you to help me find this person. Keep an eye out for any humans entering our land. I don't know if they're dangerous, so no need to hurt them but let us know. Also, I'm sure you have heard about the carvings in the woods?" People glanced around at each other and some nodded. Others looked confused and unaware.

"I'll tell you what they said and this way you're aware of what's going on. The first was Lions and Wolves, Oh my... The second: Down the windy path the lion walks."

More murmurs from the crowd. Nobody said anything directly to her so she waited a moment while they quieted down.

"Clearly, these are aimed at the pack and pride. It's a shame because both are walking a fine line between peace and war." She watched the women and several men nod their anger. Good, they realized how bad that was. "Someone smelling of chemicals is entering our land and leaving these notes."

She glanced at a few different faces, making eye contact and willing them to help. "Our people don't need anyone from outside creating problems when we are looking to live a peaceful life." Everyone nodded at that. "You can help.

Please be vigilant and let Remy, Azai, Jed or me know if you know or see anything."

The women in front of her glanced at each other then they slowly turned away. Some smiled at her, several nodded, one stopped in the crowd and turned to her. The young lady wasn't happy. "A lion cannot rule a pack of wolves."

"Valerie," Azai said from where he stood, giving her a warning snarl. Valerie narrowed her eyes then stomped to a truck, started it up and peeled out, scattering gravel.

Azai sighed. "They might as well get used to the fact you are a lioness mated to a wolf. An alpha at that. Things won't change on this end."

Remy and Jed clapped when she turned to face them. Jed had a huge grin on his face and Remy nodded in agreement.

"That's one impressive mate you have there, Azai," Remy said, his voice full of respect. She'd done it mainly to get everyone to help, but at the same time show the people Azai wasn't mated to a coward. He was an alpha and needed someone to stand as strong as him.

"She sure is," Jed said.

Remy raised his brows. "Very well done, Dali."

She smiled. "Thanks."

"You earned the women's respect from both sides. I would wager you just pushed our peace talks that much closer to being a foregone conclusion," Remy said. "Very well done. Thank you." Remy nodded and walked off the porch.

SEVENTEEN

A zai couldn't believe his woman had, in a matter of minutes, united a pack and a pride by giving them a common enemy. Now they'd have something to focus on. Something besides each other. She was brilliant and he couldn't have gotten any luckier.

"You amaze me," he whispered behind her.

She turned and gave him a warm smile. He didn't know how it was possible, but he loved her. His mate. Not just for her external beauty, but for her strength, her honesty, her genuineness. He especially loved that she saw them as a team and truly believed they could do anything together, overcome anything. If that wasn't a real partner, he didn't know what was. He almost fucked up the best thing to happen to him.

"Excuse me, ma'am," someone said from behind them. "Bertha sent me back. She said she found something, and you needed to see it right away."

They both turned to find a young lioness standing in front of them.

Azai grabbed Dalissa's hand and started after the young lioness. "Show us the way, please. Jed, find Remy, he couldn't have gone too far."

"Do you know what she found?" Dalissa called to the lion who looked over her shoulder and shook her head. "I was at the back of the group as we headed home. Bertha was first and spotted something ahead of us. She sent most home and me back to get you."

Azai looked ahead to where Bertha waited for them "You didn't get far before you had to come back. That's not reassuring. Whatever this is, someone got really close to the pack."

"You're right. Someone left a present, and by the smell, it's for you, ma'am." As they got closer, Dalissa stopped and stared at the ground. In front of them was a stuffed lion. It was gutted with stuffing spread all over the place.

"I don't smell blood." She frowned. "It smells like...paint? And something else. Not human and not shifter."

Azai squatted and picked up a piece of fluff. "Red paint. Someone wanted it to look like they killed the lion. Bertha, did you look around to see if there was anything else?"

Bertha shook her head. "Nah, I sent the lions home and waited for you."

Azai nodded. "Thank you, Bertha, we will make sure Remy knows how helpful you were. You can go on home if you want."

Bertha grunted and walked away.

"She's quite the character isn't she. Azai, I'm going to walk around and see if I find anything else. How far are we from the marked trees?"

"Not far," he replied. "They're just over there." He pointed, but it didn't help her with directions.

Dalissa took a few steps away and started in a circle. It wasn't until she did a few wider turns that she noticed something new. The chemical smell from the other notes was not evident. She glanced up, searching for her man. "Azai, no chemicals, but the scent of someone is here."

"I can explain that at least," her mate said. "That smell is the same on the note."

"I didn't smell anything on the note," she said thinking back.

"Damn, woman, you're not going to let me

112

get away with anything. Okay, you're right. The note didn't have a smell, but the money given to the kid had this smell. When Remy and I talked to the kid, he showed us the bills."

"So this was my stalker, then?" Chills ran down her legs. "It smells recent." Dalissa kept walking and picked at a piece of paper tucked into a tree branch.

"Azai. I found a note over here. It says: 'Why did you ignore my warning? You will pay for ignoring me. Go home now or else.'"

Azai growled motioning her over. "Let's go. You don't have to hide, but you aren't sitting out here in the open. This stalker is obviously crazy. They upped the ante fast and gutted a lion that we can assume represents you."

Dalissa sighed and walked over to Azai. "Okay, I'll go back to the house with you, but get someone to clean this up. We don't want any cubs wandering around and finding it."

He grabbed her shoulder, raising a hand to cup her jaw. "Dalissa, do you want to stay with me here?" He hated even asking, but he loved her and wanted her safe. "Is there anyone back home who's going to miss you?"

Her family had been weighing heavily on his mind. Could he ask her to give up her planet, family and friends to live with him here on Earth?

Was he being unfair?

She sighed and her shoulders dropped. "My family and I don't get along well. They think I'm weak and not a true shifter since I am so much smaller than anyone else. As for friends, I'll miss Zaria, but she's from Earth so I'm sure I will see here again. There's not really anyone else to miss me."

He didn't miss the sadness in her voice. It hurt him that her family had made her feel less worthy. His mate was more than any other female out there. She was perfect. "You have a family here now. Jed is already treating you like a long-lost sister. Remy was impressed and you seemed to have won over the females of my pack. It won't take long before you're fully comfortable and bossing everyone around."

Her laugh filled the air and he smiled. She was his everything and it happened so suddenly, he hadn't even realized it. If she said she wanted to go back to Aurora, he would have followed her. Hell, he would take the pack with him if she wanted.

They walked slowly toward the house. "Azai, could you introduce me to all the pack? I want to get to know them."

He sensed that was important to her. To make her feel part of them and fit in. He'd do anything to make her happy. "Sure, we can walk

114

around. It would give me a chance to see how they react to your presence. If someone from my pack is behind the notes on the tree, they won't take kindly to a lion in our midst."

He started humming.

She gaped at him. "What are you singing?"

He laughed. "I assume you aren't familiar with the movie *The Lion King*?" She shook her head and walked ahead of him. "No worries, my love. We are going to have to remedy that soon."

He trailed behind her. The closer they got to the center of pack land, the more wolves came out to stare at her. He hung back a bit and watched to see what they would do and what she would do.

She stopped and turned watching as everyone gathered around her. Impressive. He was pretty sure the whole pack had turned up. Dalissa turned to glance at him and he shrugged. She wanted to be accepted so he would stay back. His wolf wasn't happy, but she wanted this and he was going to try his damnedest not to jump in and force them to accept her.

No one spoke, they all just stared at her. Finally, she broke the silence.

"Hi, everyone. I wanted to meet you all, but this wasn't quite what I had in mind." She shifted from foot to foot, appearing unsure of what to say.

From the back of the circle, she saw movement. They parted and Jed walked through laughing.

She shook her head and sighed. "Somehow this makes much more sense."

Azai relaxed, Jed was behind this, whatever the hell it was. No one would hurt her, so he was content to watch the show.

EIGHTEEN

Dalissa had no idea what was happening, why were they staring at her.

"A-weema-weh, a-weema-weh…"

Dalissa spun around and looked at the wolves around her. Everyone was singing a weird song. She glanced at Azai and he laughed. Apparently, he understood what was going on.

They continued singing. She spun around to see Jed walking around her inside the circle of wolves singing. She started laughing when the words registered in her head. Was this a weird welcome to the pack type of thing?

"A-weema-weh, a-weema-weh…"

The wolves hummed this phrase over and

over. Dalissa couldn't stop laughing.

The wolves trailed off and everyone got really quiet. Dalissa didn't know what to do. Should she say something or let them?

"Thank you, everyone. That was a lovely song. Some of you should be trying out for *So You Think You Can Sing*."

Everyone laughed and she grinned.

Azai wrapped his arm around her waist and pulled her into his side. "I'm proud of this pack. Thank you for accepting my mate."

She nodded excitedly. "I'm honored you accept me as one of yours. I look forward to getting to know you all."

Jed stepped forward and Dalissa turned to look at him. "All but you. I owe you one for this."

Jed laughed and threw his arms wide "Word got around about you including the women in the hunt for the intruder, even about the acceptance of the lions. They wanted you to know they appreciate what you did and are trying to do."

The entire pack got down on one knee, displaying their neck in a show of vulnerability. They trusted her. Then, they stood, walked past them and nodded at Azai and at her. She tried not to cry but she had never felt accepted by anyone. These people who barely knew her did what her parents couldn't. Dalissa stood there until every wolf had walked by her. Once everyone was gone, she wrapped her arms around Azai and whispered into his ear. "Bite me now. I want the world to know we are mates."

Azai growled and picked her up. He took a few steps toward the house when they heard a voice clear their throat behind them.

"I'm really sorry to interrupt," Jed said. "But Remy just sent word, another note has been found. And a body."

Azai growled and put her down. She wanted to growl at him too. She was ready to jump on Azai and Jed poured cold water on them.

"Is it a wolf or a lion?" Azai snarled, still obviously annoyed they were interrupted.

Dalissa hadn't even thought about the ramifications of finding a body, she had been too far gone in a lust-filled haze.

"Neither. Don't know what it is."

Oh, fuck!

Azai swore under his breath and stomped toward Jed. "Let's go now."

Dalissa followed them back to the area where the last two trees had been desecrated. Remy and another lion stood by the tree staring down at something. Her lion wanted out to search the area. She was tired of someone threatening her mate and her family. Why were they all so worried? They needed to just kick some ass and if they weren't going to, she would. She'd show whoever was doing this who was the baddest bitch in town.

Azai walked around the tree and looked up at the note then down to the body below it. Dalissa marched up behind him and glanced down first. She couldn't help her eyes were drawn to the dead person. The first thing she noticed was his hand pinned by an empty syringe to the trunk. Under his hand was a scrap of paper.

"What does it say?" she asked.

Remy said, "Here's your guy. You can thank me later."

Dali took a deep breath then coughed. The acid compound covered her tongue. "He's coated in that shit. Can't smell any of him. I can't even tell if he's human." Then she noted the red stains on his hands. "How did he die? I don't smell any blood."

Dalissa stood to read the other note left on the tree: *Two groups walk a fine line, can peace be obtained, or will bloodshed win out.*

Remy paced, kicking broken limbs on the ground. "Dammit, at first I thought this was about us getting along, then maybe it was just us moving here. Now I am thinking it's more than our people. Someone wants us to fight and is trying to cause issues. The second note aimed at us and might have gotten the wolves blaming us if it wasn't for Dalissa soothing tensions at least."

She was proud of her small role in helping out Remy and Azai, but she didn't think she did as much as they claimed she had.

"Doesn't matter now. Our tree writer and my stalker is dead," she said, so ready to move past this hassle.

"Hold on a second," Azai said. "Remy, did any of your people see or hear anything?" Azai glanced at Jed to see if their people had reported anything. Most of the pack had been gathered around her singing a minute ago. That would've been a good opportunity for someone to sneak in.

"No, and we were patrolling. So someone in one of our groups caught the man here and killed him. But why not take credit for it?" Remy paced back and forth, his brow creased in concentration. Dali stood and walked around the tree while Jed watched her.

She said, "Maybe they don't want any special acknowledgment. Just doing what a pack member should to keep everyone safe. I don't smell any other shifters except for us here. Whoever killed him didn't do it here." Dalissa cocked her head at Jed. "Why are you staring at me?"

Jed shook his head. "Sorry, I was just thinking. This started just before you came."

"It was only hours before you arrived," Remy said. "Are we sure the first note wasn't put there for you to read as soon as you got here?"

Azai walked over and stood next to Jed. "It seems too much of a coincidence to be two different people, but anything is possible."

"I want to say it's one person doing both to scare Dalissa," Remy said.

"Why," she asked.

"Someone doesn't want a lion mated to a wolf," Remy replied.

She frowned, staring at the body again. The female named Valerie came to mind. She recalled what the woman said before she left in her truck. And a truck was where the first chemical trail led to.

Azai glanced at Jed and nodded. "I'll call and meet the human authorities at the road. We will show them the letters you received, the ripped-up lion, and now this body. Without being able to smell him, I don't feel comfortable messing with something we have no idea about."

NINETEEN

Anger exploded in Azai's chest, clouding his vision in a haze of red. Someone killed the stalker and he didn't get to find out why he was watching his mate. Pissed he was dead on his land and pissed someone was trying to start a fight between the wolves and lions. Now they had to bring humans onto their land which would muddy the waters even more.

It wasn't long before they heard the rustling of footsteps through the underbrush; humans were close. Most didn't know how to move through the underbrush quietly. They weren't predators.

"Mr. Whittip, I'm Detective Padding. I hear you have some problems out here and need our assistance." Azai looked at the man discreetly, his name fit. He was a portly man with thinning hair.

Azai nodded at the man. "This is my mate, Dalissa Furr. Remy Leandros is the alpha of the lion pride whose land borders mine."

The detective wrote down notes. "Your man told me you were having some issues out here with a stalker and someone leaving notes. Now you found this person, dead under a new note. Did I get that right?"

Azai grunted. "You summed it up perfectly. We don't know if he's human or not."

Dalissa turned her head away. Azai assumed she was trying not to grin at his curt reply.

The detective turned to her. "Ma'am, the first note you received was the one that was delivered to you here?"

Azai wanted to answer the questions for her and keep her out of the cop's eyes but he couldn't do that, and it wouldn't be fair to her either.

She smiled sweetly and nodded. "Yes, I had just arrived in town that morning. Azai was sent by a friend to show me around town and be my guide."

Remy coughed behind the detective and turned to look at the woods away from them. Azai was impressed with how skillfully she told the truth but left out information not pertinent to the case.

"Right before I left to meet Dalissa, Remy and I met up here to discuss the minor issues our respective groups were having. We found a phrase carved into a tree we believe was put there for her to see when she arrived."

The detective turned shrewd eyes onto the body then up at the note on the tree. "This is the third note on the tree correct?"

Azai sighed and walked closer to the detective "Yes, the first said, Lions and Wolves, Oh my... The second was: down the windy path the lion walks. And now the third note: two groups walk a fine line, can peace be obtained, or will bloodshed win out."

Detective Padding squatted his considerable girth down next to the man who lay at their feet. "What is the significance of the red paint on his hands?"

Jed stepped forward. "The stuffed animal I mentioned that was ripped open. The stuffing was covered in red paint. Azai and Remy asked some pack members to stand guard and not move anything after we found the body."

Jed looked up at Azai and he nodded.

"My mate is a lion shifter. We are wolf shifters." He curled his hands into fists in frustration. "One other thing, Detective Padding,

Dalissa has a highly sensitive nose and she smells chemicals on the body. The notes on the trees also smelled of chemicals."

The detective's brow raised. "Let me get this straight. This person had paint on his hands relating him to the stuffed animal, and the chemical smell connects him to the notes on the trees, right?" They nodded.

The detective stood and glanced behind him to a patrol man. "Get CSU out here to pick up the body and check for any chemical residue on him and the tree, please." Then he turned to Azai. "Could you have a few people out here watching the perimeter until my team shows up? I'd like to see the note and the lion toy, please. If you and Ms. Furr would accompany me, I'd appreciate that."

Azai nodded to the detective "Jed, get Markus to work the perimeter with you. Remy, want to bring in a couple of your people to help?"

Remy smiled wide and nodded. "Great idea. Let them start working together now."

"Follow me, Detective. My mate and I will be happy to show you everything we have." Azai tried to keep the bite out of his voice but he was not thrilled to be working with outsiders. He wanted to end this on his terms and not by throwing someone in jail. His wolf howled in agreement.

The detective turned back to his mate. "Dalissa, may I call you that? Where are you from? You mentioned you had just arrived and Azai was your guide."

Azai didn't like the familiarity the detective was showing his mate. It may just be curiosity as his job, but his wolf was itching to get out and show him who she belonged to.

Dalissa squeezed his hand gently and gave him a half smile. "I'm from up north. I hadn't been to this part of the country, so Gerri Wilder of the Paranormal Dating Agency helped me find Azai. They're old friends, so he agreed to show me around. Hazard of her job, she, of course, picked the one person who was fated to be mine."

The detective nodded. "You didn't get any notes or sense anyone following you on your way down here?"

"No, but when you read the first note, you will see. I think this man saw me at Gerri's apartment, if not sooner, and followed us out here." She shrugged.

Azai smirked at the detective, his mate was amazing. She gave more than asked, but less than needed.

"Detective, you should see the stuffing spread out on the ground just ahead. It covered a pretty big area. Like he was just tossing it into the air." The detective nodded and kept walking. "Please stay here, we don't want to contaminate the scene any more than you already have."

This time is was Dalissa who growled. Azai squeezed her hand. This detective was a condescending prick, and if he wasn't careful, he would be dealing with a pissed off wolf and lion.

Azai turned her toward him and nuzzled her neck. He wanted to distract her and remind her of what was happening as soon as they got some alone time. He was not waiting any longer to claim his mate. "I can't wait to get you home and have you ride my cock," he whispered. "I've been fantasizing about your breasts bouncing in my face. You lifting and dropping your slick, hot pussy on me."

Dalissa groaned and glanced around to make sure nobody was watching, then she reached down to rub his cock through his pants.

"You're going to make me crazy," she moaned softly.

"We can be crazy together," he growled, nipping her lips.

She leaned into him. "I want to taste you so badly. Every inch of you. I want you to bite me and I need to mark you. To bite you. Make us one, Azai. You, deep inside me. I'll never grow tired of it."

Azai groaned and rubbed his body against her hand. When he couldn't take it any longer, he growled and turned to face the human. "Detective, it's been a long day. I'm taking my mate home. You can meet us there when you're done here and we'll give you the notes."

Azai whistled and one of his wolves trotted out of the woods behind them. "When the detective is finished, bring him to my house. Make it at least an hour from now, but if you can give us longer, we'll take it."

Dalissa giggled and started running home. Azai chased after her. He loved watching her run, her ass giggled just enough to make his cock thicken more.

TWENTY

She reached the front door and he followed her in and pulled her into his arms and consumed her with a kiss so hot, it made her skin sizzle. The kiss was hard and rough. It invaded her senses. He caressed down her spine, farther to her hips, and settled on her ass.

He grabbed her cheeks and lifted her off the ground. Her pussy ended up level with his cock. He stroked his denim-covered shaft into the seam of her pussy. An explosion of passion took hold, leaving her breathless and panting. She rubbed her nipples over his chest.

He put her on her feet and cupped her face with his hands. His gaze spoke of passion, possession, and a feeling she knew lived in her heart for him, love. "Dalissa, I love you. There are no words to tell you how much."

Happiness unfurled in her heart between the kisses he rained on her lips and face. When he let go of her head, she curled her arms around his neck and rubbed her nose on his smooth jaw.

"There's no other man or wolf for me...just you." She licked his chin and nibbled on his neck. "You're my mate, and I'm yours. We just need to make it official."

She grazed her teeth over the galloping pulse on his throat. "Bite me, baby."

She raked her nails down his chest and lifted his T-shirt. All those clothes had to come off immediately. She tugged on the material and growled. It was taking too damn long to get him undressed. He chuckled. He tore the offensive fabric from his body, and she sighed.

He dipped his head and kissed her. Another wave of ferocious mating of the tongues and lips.

Urgency to have him in her body pushed her to open his jeans, shove her hand down, and grab his cock in a tight grip. His breath hissed out in a groan. She pushed the jeans down and pumped his shaft in a slow glide from root to tip.

"God, Dalissa. You're so fucking hot." His deep gravelly voice heightened her desire.

"Fuck me, Azai," she whimpered. "Fuck me.

Mate me. Make me yours."

He growled, toed off his jeans, and picked her up in his arms and carried her up the stairs, never releasing her mouth. He laid her on the bed carefully, as if she were a porcelain doll. They kissed again, softer, but still just as needy. She spread her legs for him and summoned him with the crook of a finger.

Heat swelled inside her. He inhaled and licked his lips. "You smell delicious." Lust shot down to her wet folds. He groaned. "And I just know you're going to taste even better."

He pounced on the bed, wrapped his arms around her legs, and immediately fastened his lips around her clit. Her hands flew to the short spikes of his hair. He swiped his thick tongue mercilessly over her clit.

She writhed and thrashed on the bed. "Yes, yes, yes, yes, yes..."

He thrust two digits into her sex and curved them inside her pussy, tickling her G-spot at the same time he grazed his teeth over her clit. A spasm took hold, and she shattered so fast, it left her breathless.

Lost to the throes of her climax, she screamed his name.

He flipped her onto her stomach, ass high in the air and legs wide. He fondled her pussy, sliding his fingers in, out, and around her wet folds. She gasped, passion tightening her nipples and making her pussy clench. She glanced over her shoulder. He bit his lip and caressed her ass with what looked like adoration.

She groaned and hung her head. Holding the sheets in a death grip, she moaned as the broad head of his cock penetrated her slick heat. He gripped her hips, stretching her pussy walls until he was balls-deep inside her.

Looking for more than just penetration, she wiggled and whimpered at the fantastic feel of his cock grazing her from inside. He tightened his hold on her hips, pulled back, and thrust into her in a fast slide. She turned her head just as he thrust into her again. He pulled back and slammed into her harder. She groaned and fisted the sheets tighter.

"Do you like that?" He impaled her again. "Like it when I fuck you from behind?"

"Yes, yes. Please."

"Please what? What do you need, my sexy mate?" The low growl and his feral features made her pussy squeeze at his cock.

"Fuck me harder, faster. Give me more!"

His wicked grin made the heat inside her expand through every cell and nerve ending. Hair sprouted on his face. She became fascinated.

His features turned wild, untamed and almost feral with intensity. Inside her pussy, his cock thickened and grew.

"Mine," his voice claimed.

"Yes. Yours, and you're mine." Her breath hitched. She hung her head and lowered her front to lie flat on the bed just as he seemed to let go of his control.

He pulled back and hammered into her in harsh drives. Azai thrust and the pull of his thickened cock dragged loud, harsh moans out of her throat. Skin slapping skin, her moans, and his growls were the only noises in the room.

Fire filled her pussy with each slam of his cock.

"God, yes!" A ball of tension grew inside her womb. Her pussy fluttered, and her back bowed. He snarled and dropped on all fours over her, caging her. Sweat turned the slide of his body over hers into a sensual glide of flesh on flesh. He licked the back of her shoulder. She moaned and propelled back into each of his thrusts, pushing him even farther into her pussy.

He flipped her over and holding himself over her with one arm, he moved a hand between her thighs and squeezed her clit between two fingers. She gasped, tensed, and when his canines dug into her shoulder, she sat up and dug her teeth into his shoulder, her world exploded. Her pussy clenched around his cock and squeezed as she came.

He slowed the pummeling thrusts, tensed above her, and snarled while still biting her shoulder. Hot semen filled her womb in multiple jerks. He continued to come for long moments with his teeth still embedded in her flesh and hers in his.

Attached, they fell to the side on the mattress. He wrapped his hands around her waist, his cock jerked in her pussy, and he licked at her shoulder. She panted air into her lungs, licked his shoulder and closed her eyes.

"Don't go to sleep, my love, the detective could show up anytime." Dalissa groaned. "I love you, furball, but I can't handle it. I'm ready to pass out. I need my energy for round two tonight."

Azai groaned and slapped her on the ass. "Furball was the best you could come up with?"

Dalissa grinned "My movie knowledge is sadly lacking. I will talk to Remy to see if he can suggest some suitable nicknames for a wolf. But you win, dibs on the shower, and no, you can't join me, or we will never get out before he shows up."

TWENTY-ONE

A zai walked into the guest room to take a fast shower, his mind kept drifting back to the last ninety minutes with his mate. His cock thickened and he groaned and turned the water on cold.

Ten minutes later, he was dressed and heading down the stairs, just in time to see the detective walking up to the porch. Azai opened the door before he could knock and gestured for him to come in.

"Can I get you a cup of coffee, Detective Padding?" Azai ushered him into the kitchen and the table. "Dalissa will be with us in just a few minutes."

"Coffee would be great, thank you. Tell me,

have your wolves smelled anything unusual, anyone coming and going they aren't used to? Besides the unknown dead guy."

"That's part of the problem. Remy's pride just moved in not long ago. We are still getting used to whose land ends where. The wolves wouldn't attribute a smell as out of ordinary because the lions have been on our land."

"I understand that but wouldn't that only leave you with the scents of the lions? So, you're saying only wolves and lions have been across your land?"

Azai looked at the detective with new eyes. "I see you're familiar with shifters then; some shifters are made up of more than just one type. So, we wouldn't find it odd to find a scent other than wolves or lions. We don't know enough about the lion's pride yet to determine if there are other shifters living with them. My mate, for instance, is a lion living in a pack of wolves. Her scent will mingle with ours."

The detective rubbed his hand across his face and sighed "I figured as much. The area is now clear, and your wolves are free to roam again."

"Detective, here are the notes I received."

Detective Padding jumped slightly in his seat. He apparently hadn't heard Dalissa approaching from behind.

He flushed a light red and took the paper from her. Azai watched as he read the notes. The man mouthed every word to himself. It was quite annoying and just another reason his wolf wanted to eat him.

"Well, they seem pretty straight forward, if your person hadn't killed him, he would probably have escalated and attacked you, ma'am. It's a typical stalker scenario, of course, being a shifter I'm sure you could have handled it on your own."

Dalissa leaned back against his chest. He was ready to toss the detective out for the way he spoke to her and she knew it. The mate bond strengthened the longer she stood next to him. He could feel her joy and contentment being near him.

"I'm taking these with me. I will let you know if we hear anything else on the body or chemicals. Other than that, seems your problems are solved." The detective got up and walked toward the door. "How far am I from my car, by the way?"

Behind him, Azai heard Dalissa snort.

"If you walk to the right you will find the road, then you're about a half mile from the entry point into the woods you used."

The detective huffed and walked outside. "Whose truck is that? Any chance I could get a ride to my car?"

Azai stared at the man for a moment. "I'll grab my keys and be right with you." Azai shut the door and stalked back into the kitchen. "Do you think he's being rude because we are shifters or just because he's a douche?"

She burst into laughter and just shook her head. "Hurry back. Now that this mystery is all solved, I want to go for a run, just the two of us."

"You read my mind. There's much of our land you haven't seen yet. Tonight, we hunt together."

* * *

Megan slipped on her fuck-me shoes and checked her makeup one last time. Then she grabbed the keys to the truck. "Turner, get your ass over here." She waited as the brainless, zombie-like guy shuffled toward her. His eyes never focused on anything, yet he never tripped or hit walls. She was thrilled she finally got the recipe correct.

"Get in your truck. Passenger side." She locked the back door then walked on the balls of her feet through the rocky driveway. Fuck. She hated doing shit like this, but it was the best and fastest way to collect a lot of men at one time.

When she came upon the bar and grill that

several of the wolf shifters stopped at every night after work, she cooked up the plan to start the revolution. This was why she loved living so close to the wolves.

She cranked the truck and backed it out of the garage, careful not to hit her car pulled to the side. Turner sat quietly, staring out the windshield. He'd been the fifth test shifter for the zombie drug she had worked on for years.

On the first two, the drug fried their brains. Smoke came out of the pores in the scalp. The third shifter had his cranium tissue ooze out his nose and ears. The fourth was close, but it didn't obey orders; it was strictly a vegetable. And Turner was perfect. A massive wolf at her command.

They pulled into the bar parking lot and found a spot in the second row. From a plastic baggy on the seat, she took out two small containers filled with her own ketamine mixture. It was basically a date rape drug but powerful enough that a sprinkle would kill a human. She shoved those into her clutch along with several small syringes filled with zombie juice and snapped it closed.

She stepped out and looked at the flood light illuminating that area. "Turner, get out and throw a rock to break the bulb."

He climbed out, immediately picking up a

stone and launching it into the air. And damn, if he didn't get it on the first try. Glass shattered and plummeted to the ground. The area became dark.

"Wait in the truck and listen carefully for me to call you." As she started for the building entrance, a truck drove in and parked. First victim of the night. She hurried toward the driver when he climbed from the truck. His eyes widened seeing her. She took a whiff. Wolf with that damn factory smell.

"Sir," she said, "could you help me?" Having reached him, she placed a hand on his forearm and leaned forward exposing large amounts of cleavage. "I'm having car trouble."

His eyes traveled exactly where she wanted. "Sure, young lady."

Megan took his hand and led him into the darker area.

He asked, "Are you part of the lion pride moving next to our pack?"

"Yes," she replied, then pointed to a car, "There's my car." Stopping, she released his hand and opened her purse. "Go on. I need to find my keys."

The wolf continued toward the car. She said in a low voice, "Turner, get ready." The wolf turned.

"Did you say something?"

She smiled. "I said I should've been ready, with my keys out. Here they are." She lifted the truck keys from the small purse and jangled them. She hurried toward him as he began walking. Her fingers nimbly exchanged the keys for the injection.

"What seems to be the problem, miss?"

She came up behind him, "Well, you know — " she rammed the short needle into the back of his arm.

He jerked around. "Ow, what the fu — " Immediately, the wolf leaned against the car, knees giving way.

"Turner, now." With lightning speed, he rounded the car. "Cover his mouth." She pointed to the man falling to the ground. Turner wrapped his large hands over the guy's face and held tightly as the body thrashed then slowly went still. "Put him in the back of the truck."

The man was limp as if made with no bones. Once again, she headed for the bar entry. That was much easier than this morning when she spotted a man walking through a breakfast shop parking lot. The moment she stuck in the needle, the man jerked, spilling coffee down the front of her shirt.

Turner still got him into the truck, but she cut that search short and focused on tonight when most of the male wolves would be at this bar. Men were so predictable. Show them beer or boobs and they were under your control.

A man walked out, and she sniffed. "Sir, could you help me?" The same script played out with the same ending. She figured they could get three victims in the back seat of the truck and around six in the bed if they lay on top of each other.

Shit. She forgot to tell Turner to make sure the tarp covered the bodies. A car pulled in with a man and woman. She hid behind a truck until they were inside. Then another truck pulled in. Damn. This was easier than she thought.

When she'd reached capacity, they went back to the house where all the zombies followed her order to wait in the room downstairs with her coffee wolf.

For the second round, she took one of the wolves along with Turner. He would make the perfect bait to draw his friends to her when they walked out of the bar. In the meantime, she'd have to get in with the men and drug their beers, then when each wolf got drowsy, she'd walk them to their — her — vehicle.

It would be a long and productive night.

TWENTY-TWO

Azai walked back into the house after driving the police detective to his car and called out for Dalissa. She padded out of the kitchen, on four legs. Azai stopped and stared. She was amazing in her lion form. Her golden fur made him want to run his hands across her body. Who was he kidding? He always wanted to do that, no matter her form. Azai reached back and opened the front door. "Okay, baby, give me a minute to shift and I'm right behind you."

Azai watched her trot outside and stop on the porch. She looked so regal sitting there, looking at everyone and everything around her. He quickly stripped and shifted and joined her.

Can you hear me, love?

She turned her head and looked at him then leaped off the porch. *I guess that was a yes. Are you taking the lead, or do you want me to show you around?*

Show me our land. I want to see it all with you.

They ran all over the acreage, chasing rabbits and squirrels and each other. Occasionally Azai would cut behind her and nip her hind leg and take off. She retaliated by bumping into him and pushing him around. *Azai where are we going?* He carefully steered her in certain directions as they ran, she let it go for a bit, but she was curious what he had planned.

Yes, it's time to see more of your new home. I hope you aren't afraid of heights.

They broke out of the trees and Jed walked toward them. "I left a backpack with some clothes for you two just behind those trees." Jed pointed to the left of where they were standing. "After you are done, just leave them in the area and someone will grab them later. Enjoy your evening." Jed smiled and walked away. Dalissa watched him for a moment then trotted over to the trees to find the clothes. She was really curious to see what Azai had planned.

A few minutes later, they were both fully dressed and standing under a set of stairs that led to a platform far above their heads. "Azai, what is this?" Dalissa craned her head back and stared.

145

"We are going zip lining. Ready to fly like a bird?" Azai laughed and Dalissa gaped at him. Was he serious? Her lion didn't seem to be upset by the prospect so that was a plus. "All right I trust you. Lead the way, darling."

Halfway up the stairs, Dalissa stopped and stared out across the land. "This is the most beautiful sight I have ever seen. So many shades of green and the sky is on fire."

He snuggled up behind her on the step. "Our sunsets are amazing. You can't imagine all the colors the eye can see. It's breathtaking."

"On Aurora, the skies are stunning, but seldom vary in hues," she commented.

"Why's that, I wonder?"

"Since the universe is created out of the same basic elements, our planets would share a lot of characteristics. But it's other particles in the air that create the different colors."

"Like what," he asked. "What do we have in the air that's different than yours?"

She became a bit sheepish. "Well, it sounds bad to say, but what we've discovered in many places on your planet is that air pollution messes with the elements' purity, altering it."

"You seem to know a lot of scientific stuff."

She shrugged. "It's normal learning in our

education system. We study the composition and elemental make up of everything on our planet. This helps with maintaining natural resources and understanding how to prevent ecological disasters. I had some advanced schooling in what you call chemistry and found it so fascinating."

She turned back to the setting sun. "It's hard to believe something so beautiful could exist."

"No really," he replied. "I see amazing beauty every time I look at you."

She laughed. "Do women on Earth actually go for that line?"

He lifted and dropped a shoulder. "Don't know. Never said that to anyone before."

Dalissa glanced at Azai, tears filling her eyes. "Thank you for sharing this with me."

Azai leaned close to her. "There is more. Keep climbing, love." With a regretful sigh, she turned away from the view and climbed the stairs, the wood under her hand still held the warmth from the day's sun. The breeze gently moved her hair and brought her Azai's scent. This was the perfect evening.

Finally, they reached the top and Dalissa turned in a circle. There was too much beauty, she couldn't even take it all in. "Ma'am, if you will come this way, we will get you strapped in and ready for your trip." Dalissa spun around and stared at the man standing behind her. In his hands, he had some kind of gear. Dalissa glanced at Azai and saw he was already strapped in and waiting on her. He eyed the man in front of her. She was sure if his hands strayed Azai would be out of his harness in a heartbeat.

They stood at the end of the platform and Dalissa looked out. "Azai, I'm ready to fly with you." She smiled at him and stepped off. The wind chafed her cheeks as they flew. She reached out into the air around her and laughed in delight.

To her side, she could hear Azai howling, and she tossed her head back and did the same. Her laughter rang through the air and tears poured from her eyes. To soon the platform loomed ahead of them. She took one last look around and tried to memorize everything she saw.

As she landed on the platform, she said, "I saw a cabin. Is that part of your pack way out here?"

Azai nodded. "That's Turner Lupin's place."

"Why so far away from everyone else?"

He sighed. "Turner had issues with playing well with others. He argued a lot and had a hot temper to boot. He felt more comfortable alone. So he came out this way."

"You said all that in past tense. Is he not there anymore?" she asked.

Azai's brows pushed down. "About three months ago, he disappeared."

"Where did he go?"

He shrugged. "Don't know. His truck and some clothes were gone, so we assumed he decided he didn't want to belong to the pack anymore and went out on his own."

"Is that normal here?" she asked.

"Disappearing isn't, but living away from the main pack is somewhat common. The highly opinionated who don't back down are usually the ones."

Dali thought back to Megan living away from the pack. The woman was definitely opinionated on the order of the food chain.

"You ready for the next section?" he asked.

"Come on, man," she smiled, "you're holding up the line."

When they reached the last platform and climbed down, Dalissa's cheeks hurt from laughing and the smiles.

"Thank you again Azai for letting me fly. I never expected to do it or love it." Dalissa raced down the stairs and into the grassy area. Her arms thrown wide, she spun in a circle.

"I'm thankful I could give you that. Are you ready to shift and feel the wind in your fur?"

Dalissa smiled and walked behind the trees to shift again. *I loved the air but want to feel the leaves under my feet again. Lions are meant for the land, and you are meant to be beside me. Let's run for a bit, love.*

They ran for another hour or so. Dalissa explored and learned the land around her new home. There was so much to see and smell, she couldn't ever get bored.

Are you ready to head home, sweetheart? The front door is open and it's getting dark. We don't want mosquitoes biting our naked asses later.

I'll race you home. Loser has to come second.

Oh, it was on. Azai ran as fast as his wolf would allow; he swore he wanted to lose.

They were neck and neck coming to the house. Both leapt for the porch, Dali shifting midair, then tucking into a somersault to land on her feet. He slid to a stop, jaw hanging down.

That was too cool, baby. You gotta teach me that.

"Sure," she said out loud, smiling. "That's normal where I come from. For the younger generations, anyway. The older ones like the less active version." She stepped forward, opened the door, and waved him in. "I wish to be the loser. Now shift and show mama her lollipop."

Oh, shit. He hated getting hard in his wolf form, but luckily it morphed along with the rest of his body. This would be a long night.

TWENTY-THREE

Just as the sun came up, Dalissa woke to banging downstairs. She groaned, but she wasn't too upset since her mate was wrapped around her, keeping her warm.

Jed's voice filtered through the door. "Alpha, we got a problem."

Azai moaned. "When don't we anymore?"

She reached around and tapped his bare ass. "Come on, *Alpha*. This is your job."

He leaned forward and nuzzled her neck. "Can I quit and stay in bed with you all day?"

She snorted. "In your dreams."

"Alpha!" Jed hollered.

"All right, Jed. We're coming down." They threw the covers back and rolled out. Dali put on a robe while Azai shuffled on a pair of pants. "I'll kill him if this anything less than a real emergency."

She smacked his backside. "Quit complaining and get your cute ass down there." She followed him to the first floor but hung back and watched from the kitchen since she wasn't dressed. She wanted to get the gist of the conversation then hop in the shower.

The front door opened. "All right, Jed, what do you have for us now?"

Jed rubbed the back of his head and looked around. "Did you see Remy on your run last night or this morning?"

"No, I haven't seen him since we left you at the body last night. Why? What happened?"

"Bertha showed up this morning. No one has seen him since last night. He just disappeared."

He leaned in through the front door. "Dalissa, babe, we need your sniffer. Remy is missing. We need to go back to where the body was and see if you can track him. Jed, let me grab clothes for my mate."

Dalissa came out of the house a couple seconds later. Jed took a step back. She roared at him and sat. He said, "You're not scaring me. I was just shocked at how big you are in that form."

"Whatever you say, Jed. Let's go, baby." Azai ran his hand down Dalissa's head.

A woman out of breath came up to the porch. "You're awake, Alpha. Thank god you're here. We were afraid you were gone to."

His brows raised. "No. It's just the lion's alpha gone."

Her brows lowered. "Remy is missing too?"

Jed lifted his arms. "Hold on a minute. We're not on the same page." He turned to the woman. "Susan, who is missing that you know of?"

"All of the men," she answered.

"What?" Azai choked out.

"Well, not all of them." The woman stood, wringing her hands together. Azai gently took her hands into his. "It's only those who work at the filter facility." Dali didn't know how many that was. Several, most of the guys?

He tensed. "Tell me what you know."

"We thought the mates were just having a few extra beers and were going to be late." Susan said. "But they didn't come home. Plus, Nelda got a call from her mate's boss yesterday morning. Harry never showed up for work."

"Where is he?" Azai asked.

"She hasn't been able to reach him. He's not answering his phone."

Azai growled. "Why didn't someone come to me earlier?"

Susan tilted her head down. "Sorry, Alpha. You were busy with finding that person leaving notes, then the dead body, and when not there, you've been with your mate, uh. . . mating. We didn't want to bother you until we were sure something was wrong. You two need to be together until. . ."

Dali finished the sentence: until they were mated.

Fuck. Guilt hit her. Of all the days for things to go to hell in a handbasket. "Sorry, Susan." Azai glanced at her. If animals could blush, she would be at the moment. "Okay, give us a minute to see about Remy, then we'll talk with the ladies and Nelda."

"Oh, she's not here," Susan added. "She's driving around town looking for her mate's truck."

Her mate dragged a hand down his face. "Okay, keep the others calm. We'll be back."

What the hell was happening?

When she heard Azai take a step she jumped off the porch and took off running to the tree. She hoped the body was gone by now. She wanted to get a better smell of the elemental compounds there.

She heard the guys running behind her, but she didn't stop. She was on a mission. When she got to the area around the tree, she slowed and started searching for Remy's scent. *Azai, can you hear me like this*?

"I can hear you, Dalissa. Did you find something?"

Not Remy yet, but the chemical smell is stronger than the last time here. The person was here again.

"Jed can you hear her through the pack link?"

"Yeah, boss, I can."

"Was anyone patrolling after the police left?"

"No. We thought it was over."

I think the scent is heading in the same direction as before.

Azai said over his shoulder, "Jed, hang out here. We could be a while."

"Got it, boss."

Dalissa started following the scent. It got stronger the closer to the road they got. There were no signs of Remy being dragged. She had no idea how this person got in and left with a man the size of Remy.

When they got to the road, she searched to the left and to the right, but couldn't tell anything.

Azai, do you see anything out of the ordinary. The scent is everywhere.

Dalissa crossed the road and checked the other side. There had to be a vehicle around here somewhere. It was the only way she could think of to transport Remy.

Then she smelled it. Remy. His scent overpowered the chemical smell.

What's across the road? Whose land is it?

There's a couple houses back there. It's not shifter land. Humans own it. Why? Did you find the trail over there?

Remy's scent is strongest here. The chemical smell actually takes a back burner. Wait... come here, I think I see something on a tree.

Dalissa shifted and impatiently waited for him to cross the road, then took the backpack with her clothes.

"Is this another note, you think?" she asked, slipping on a shirt.

Azai stepped up to where she stood. Carved into the tree was the words: *No trespassing or you die.*

"Die? What the hell does that mean? You can't kill someone for that."

Azai shrugged. "Look around. See if there's anything else."

Dalissa searched and asked. "Would Remy come over here? Do you think the owner of this land killed Remy?"

Azai sighed. "We won't stop until we find him or his body. Let's keep moving but stay together."

Dalissa nodded and moved trunk to trunk. "Here's another one. Wolves and Lions aren't meant to be." Dalissa wasn't sure if they were talking about the two packs living close together or her and Azai.

"It could have started out as something between the two packs and our mating could have caused this to become something bigger."

Dalissa realized he was right. Maybe her coming here was a mistake. She cost one person their life, and possibly a second. Azai didn't take his eyes off her. Dalissa knew she was freaking out a little, but guilt was weighing heavy on her.

"Azai, is this my fault? Did I cause that guy's death, and now Remy's?"

Azai grabbed her face between his hands and brought her mouth to his. "No, this started before you got here, remember. That guy was far from innocent and Remy can handle his own. You and I became scapegoats for this maniac's own

158

agenda. You're right where you belong."

Dalissa nodded. "I hear you, I really do. My lioness agrees, but my brain is having trouble believing it."

She pulled her big girl panties up, metaphorically speaking, of course. She was the mate of the pack alpha. She needed to remember that.

"Let's go a bit farther and see if there is another message waiting for us." They walked another twenty feet into the woods and didn't see anything. "Maybe that was the last one. Let's go back and call Detective Padding."

Dalissa agreed it was the smartest move. She turned and stared at the tree in front of them. "Azai, what does that mean?"

On the tree, it read *I see you*. Before he could reply, her vision went dark and she hit the ground. She never felt Azai land next to her.

TWENTY-FOUR

A zai woke, tied to a chair, his vision blurry. His first thought was for his mate. "Dalissa, where are you?" He heard groaning behind him and tried to turn to see if it was her. "Azai is that you? What are you doing here?"

Azai couldn't believe his ears. "Remy? You're alive. "

"I'm alive but this piece of shit who took us is going to wish they had never been born when I get out of here."

Azai's sight cleared and he glanced around. Well, he thought his vision was focused. He couldn't believe what he was seeing. "Remy, what the fuck is going on? Why are all my men here and staring at nothing? And where the hell are we?" At least he knew where the males in his pack were. He was sure Susan and Nelda wouldn't find them.

"Great questions, my friend. I'd like to know the same things."

"Did you see Dalissa?"

"No. Were you together?"

"Yeah. Bertha noticed you hadn't returned home last night. Jed was at my front door at the ass crack of dawn. Dali smelled you across the road then everything is black until now."

Azai kicked the foot of one of his pack. "Hey, Thomas. Snap out of it." The man didn't flinch. Azai leaned forward. "Thomas! Thomas!"

"Give it up," Remy said. "I tried all that shit already. They are zombies. I don't know what happened to them."

Agitation setting in, Azai pulled on his hands, trying to break free. "Fuck. Is this cable?"

"By the looks of what's around your wrists, I'd say it's a half-inch wire rope with a breaking strength around ten tons."

"Fuck!" Azai thrashed in the chair. "You tied up too?"

"Tied up and not the good kind."

Azai growled in frustration. "Did you try to

cut through the cables?"

Remy snarled. "What do you think?"

He focused on shifting his hand to bring out a claw to cut at the bindings. But nothing happened. "Remy, I can't shift, can you?"

"No, I have been trying since I woke up in here. I can't even sense my lion. How about you?"

"Shit, you're right. My wolf is buried... it's the only way I can describe it. I know he's still there but it's like he's far away and I can't reach him. What the hell could do this to us?"

The door opened in front of Azai and he strained to see who stood in the doorway. "I'll tell you what could do this to you. I could."

Remy gasped. "Megan? What the hell? Why would you do this to us?"

Azai heard the shock and anger in Remy's voice.

"Who are you and what's going on?" Azai didn't really care who she was. He just wanted to know where his mate was. "What did you do with Dalissa?"

"She's okay... well, for now at least." The woman walked around Azai and stopped behind him.

"Long time no see, Remy. Did you miss me?" Azai heard the chair behind him creak as Remy moved. He tried to look over his shoulder but couldn't see anything clearly.

"No, I didn't miss you. I kicked you out of the pride because you're bat shit crazy. I should have realized you were behind these notes and carvings."

"You really should have put two and two together. Who else could have burned perfect circles into a tree and keep it alive, hmmm? Who else could have killed that filthy alien with no trace of how he died?"

"Alien?" Remy questioned.

"The guy stalking Dalissa. I don't know what he is. Never smelled anything like him. Plus, he had a gadget that made him invisible. I kept that, of course. I caught him sneaking around and decided he'd make a great red herring."

"But he smelled like that chemical stuff completely," Azai said.

"Well, duh," she replied. "I knew if you smelled him, you wouldn't put him and the notes together. So I sprayed him and dumped him there."

The chair creaked behind Azai again and he heard footsteps across the floor. In front of him, the woman called Megan stopped. "I'll be back. I have a new friend who requires my attention. Be good while I'm gone."

"Wait," Azai hollered. "What did you do to my pack?"

Megan stopped and smiled. "You and Remy are smart men. Figure it out." She turned to the men. "Everybody up, now." All but the two bound were standing in a heartbeat. "Everyone, lift your right leg." Each pack member stood stone still, looking like human flamingos. "Everyone, sit." All went down like the ceiling fell on their heads.

Megan looked at him and Remy. "Very obedient. The only kind of man to have." She walked out, closing the door with a dead thud.

Azai waited a few more minutes and then said, "Spill, Remy, who is she and why did she do this."

"Megan was my beta," Remy replied.

"Beta? Are you serious?"

"I know it's unusual for a female to hold that role, but she was the fastest and smartest. She earned the right until little things she began to do and say added up to a new world order."

"What do you mean?"

"She wanted a pure society of shifters, one where we never intermingled with other shifters. The purer, the better. We had been looking at moving here for a while and she was livid I would consider moving next to wolves. As far as she was concerned, we should take your land and keep it for ourselves. She said we were a higher class of shifter and we needed to rid the world of lesser beings."

Remy groaned and Azai didn't know what to say. Bat shit crazy fit this chick, but that made her dangerous. "So that explains why she was trying to start fights between us but explain the chemicals. That doesn't fit with what you told me so far."

"The last straw that caused me to exile her... she was experimenting on shifters. We found a warehouse that she had filled with different species — mostly non-mated males where no one would miss them much. She was trying to suppress their ability to shift. She used chemicals she could buy off the internet."

Azai groaned and pulled at the binding to the chair. "Well, I guess she figured out how to suppress the animal within. So, she used these chemicals to burn her note into the tree or a circle to get your attention?"

Remy sighed in frustration "It would seem so. I never thought she would come back around after I attempted to have her committed to an institution."

"Holy shit, Remy. This all sounds so

farfetched! How did she get us here? Would someone be working with her or is she that strong?"

"That I don't know."

"Okay," Azai said, "what about these guys? What did she do to them?"

"Don't know that either."

"Goddammit, Remy. What do you know?"

"I know I'm going to kick your ass if don't fucking chill out."

He took a deep breath and let it out slowly. "Sorry, man. These are my wolves and I can't do one thing to help them."

"I get it, but we got to think this through. If we can figure out what she's done and why, then maybe we can undo it."

Azai snorted. "She gave them some drug that made them mindless. Without a cure, they are as good as dead."

Remy sighed. "And so are we."

TWENTY-FIVE

Dalissa woke to someone calling her name. The smell of grass and dirt filled her senses. Her eyes opened to see Megan in her face.

"Dalissa, oh my god. Are you okay?" Megan helped her sit up. "What happened to you?"

She rubbed her forehead. "I'm not sure. Azai and I—" She looked around. Instead of the trees they were in, she lay in a ditch next to a smaller road. "Where's Azai?"

"I don't see him," Megan replied. "It's just you. How did you get here?"

"I don't know. Where are we?" She noted Megan's car parked in the middle of the road.

"About a mile from my house. Let's get you

settled with an ice pack for your head." Dali let Megan help her up and into her car. "Are you hurting anywhere? Broken bones?"

She shook her head then leaned back and closed her eyes. "I need to find Azai."

Megan snorted. "Even though he's a wolf, he's an alpha and can take care of himself. My question is why did he leave you behind?"

Dali sat up, brows down. "He didn't leave me behind."

Her friend glanced at her with an *are you sure?* look. "I didn't smell anyone but you. And you were with him. . ."

No. That couldn't be right. Azai would never leave her. He loved her. They were mated.

Megan sighed. "This will be a hard lesson, but you can't trust anyone but your pride. Wolves are the worst." Dali shook her head, not believing it. "I'm sorry, Dalissa."

"He's probably at the pack getting help to find me." She tried connecting to him through their link, but something was wrong. The bond wasn't there. She didn't feel him in her mind. Maybe she was too far from the pack. The only other reason keeping her from connecting would be death. A burst of panic seared through her veins.

Megan sniffed and patted her hand. "It'll be

all right, Dali. I got you, girlfriend." The car slowed and they turned onto a gravel drive to a cute craftsman-style house.

"Your home is adorable," she said. "I love the hues."

"Thank you," Megan replied. "I'm just renting. It's luck that the owner has taste in style."

Next door, a second house mimicked the first but in a peach color instead of blue. "Who lives there?" Dali asked.

"Nobody, right now. But maybe that will change soon?" Megan smiled at her with a twinkle in her eye.

What the hell did she mean by that? Dali had no intention of moving out of her mate's home.

The car stopped outside a back door. "Don't get out. Let me help you," Megan said, jumping from the car.

What a wonderful person. Dali wondered how someone so nice couldn't get along with others. Her door opened and Megan held her arm and guided her into the house. Besides a headache, she felt fine. Whatever happened she wasn't harmed.

"Here," Megan said as they approached a white sofa, "lie down here." Her friend moved the throw pillow to lie flat. When she was settled, Megan left to get her ice for her head.

The home seemed very cozy. No photos or pictures of family or friends. No knickknacks either. In fact, the place looked barely lived in. Megan walked back in.

"I don't have a proper ice bag, so I used a plastic baggie. Hope that's okay." She reached out to take it, but Megan held it. "Let me. You just stay there." She lifted her shoulders and the woman set towel-wrapped ice against the bump on the right side. "There you go." She sat in a matching upholstered chair.

"So, have you changed your mind about going home?"

Right. Megan took her to the power plant when she and Azai had their disagreement.

"Yes, we worked it out. He was worried I'd get hurt."

"Hurt how?" Megan asked.

She didn't want to go into the letters and the stalker and all that. "They had some issues that needed attention."

"Is everything all settled?"

"Yes," she answered, "the root of the problem was taken care of."

"Good," Megan said. "So, where are you from again? I'm fascinated with how strong your abilities are."

Oh shit. She was so busted. How was she to lie her way through with a shifter. "Well, I doubt you've heard of my pride. We're really far from here."

"What is the name?"

"Aurora. Ever hear of it?" So far so good.

Megan bit her bottom lip. "I don't think so." Her friend settled back in her chair. Dali groaned. That couldn't be good. "What makes you superior?"

Dali face her face heat up. "Oh, I'm not that much bet—"

"Yes, you are. You can smell things the alpha can't. I bet your vision and hearing is the same."

Shit, shit, shit. Her brain shifted into overdrive. "Perhaps my family has fewer humans in the lineage." *Like thousands of years of no humans.* "Sorta like a purer blood line. I don't know for certain." Time to change the subject. She sat up. "I'm feeling much better."

Megan popped up from the chair. "Stay there. Let me make us some tea. Or would you like something else to drink?"

"Tea would be great. Thank you." When Megan walked out, she let out a deep breath. She needed to get back to the pack and find Azai. And figure out what happened to them.

Last thing she remembered was standing across the road from pack land. She'd been hit in the head from behind. Exactly where Megan placed the ice pack. Had Dali mentioned her head pounded in the back? And how did Megan know that she could smell better than Azai. Dali never saw her around the trees where the notes were. Before she could put anything together, Megan came back.

"I have wonderful ginger tea that will calm your nerves. It's my favorite. I had some cheesy crackers, too, in case you're hungry." She set a cutting board with two glasses of tea and small saucer with crackers. "Sorry about the board. I don't entertain much and don't have nice platters."

"No problem," Dali said and picked up her tea glass. "I'm not used to that kind of stuff." And she wasn't. Technology on her planet could make food where she took a plate from the microserver.

"So," Dali asked, "in the car you mentioned something about lions being better than wolves?" She listened carefully to the reply.

Megan snorted. "Yes. Lions are the strongest, biggest shifters. No one can out do us."

"Bears are really big, and dragons."

Megan laughed. "Dragons?

Oh fuck. Did they not have dragon shifters

172

on Earth? She faked a laugh. "I'm just joking. There's no such thing as dragons here. But bears are real."

Her friend waved her off. "Bears are too slow. Lions could get away from them by walking fast. No one compares to us."

She raised her glass to take a swallow, then an idea came to her. "You know, Megs, you're exactly right. Lions are top of the line."

"Damn straight, woman." Megan took a drink. "Mmm. This is great. Try it."

Glass in hand, Dali stood and paced. "What I've seen of the wolves, they are weak and don't deserve to be here," she lifted her glass then lowered it. "They are fortunate we lions haven't overrun them."

"That's because Remy is worthless. He's no better than the other species. When I'm the alpha, the pride will be run like it should be. Like our ancestors did. Dominance over the masses."

"Absolutely, girl," Dali said. "All male alphas should step down and let the women take charge. Then things would get done right the first time. There won't be any pissing contests because lionesses outclass them all."

Megan rose from her seat and walked to her. Dali lifted her glass, but Megan's approach startled her. The lioness said, "Do you really believe that?" Meg's eyes shone with desperate hope, a silent plea for someone who believed as she did. With the woman standing beside her, a lie would be a dead giveaway. What Dali said next would either break her suspicions wide open or possible kill her.

Dali drew her brows down. "You're my only female friend here. Why would I lie to you?" Answer a question with a question. It worked every time.

Megan smiled. Surprising Dali, the woman's eyes turned glassy. "I've been waiting for someone like you for a long time."

Dali kept her poker face and calm pulse. "Me?"

"Yes. You understand how to fix this world, to make it a better place. And you have the power to back up your words. You're perfect." Megan lifted her glass in a toast. "Here's to making the world worth living in." They clinked cups and both drank to the bottom.

* * *

Standing in Megan's living room, Dali puckered like she'd swallowed a lemon. "Whoa, girl. That's a lot of ginger."

Her friend took her glass. "I like it strong. Come with me," Megan headed toward the kitchen, "I want to show you something before we run out of time."

She didn't voice her thoughts, but what time was ticking down? She followed Megan through the kitchen, out the door they came in, and to the house next door. Megan had said the house was empty. Why were they going inside?

As Megan pulled a key from her pocket, she asked, "If I told you I'd found a way to make our dreams come true, would you be interested in knowing how?"

Her friend's dreams were nothing like her own. This lady was bat shit crazy, but Dali had played along to see where it would lead, if anywhere. She was now very curious to what was going on. "You bet," she answered. "Is there a way I can help?"

Megan smiled wider. "You already are. Come on." She opened the door and they walked into a kitchen—a kitchen like none she'd ever seen. How many people had a spectrophotometer next to the oven?

The living room looked very similar to her advanced chemistry labs during her education: glass beakers, conical flasks, crucibles, graduated cylinders, pipettes, Bunsen burners and more. What was all of this for?

Then she noted containers on a metal table

along a wall. Sulfuric acid, formaldehyde, chloroform, periodic acid, phenol, calcium cyanide. What the fuck? She'd never seen such a collection of chemicals in her life. Each one could kill a human or shifter on its own. Why were they here?

Suddenly it came to her. Chemicals. Megan was the one carving on the trees and leaving the notes. But what had she created?

"Megan," her voice sounded breathless, "what have you done?" Dali noted how accusatory that seemed. She didn't need to blow this game now that she was close to the answer. "I mean, this is incredible. What have you created?"

Megan's squinted eyes relaxed and the smile returned. She picked up a clear spray bottle with *no smell* written on it. "This masks any smell. Spray this on and you will be scentless."

Except the chemical smell remained, but she wasn't reminding Megan of that. No need to help the enemy.

"Amazing," she said. "How does it work?"

"The compounds in the spray target the proteins that create the body's natural odor, eating the source basically." That was easy enough to get. There were dozens of enzymes that got rid of the odor. Anyone with a pet has a bottle or two sitting around.

"What else?"

Next, a small baggie was grabbed off a shelf. "Inhaling this in smoke form suppresses a shifters ability to shift and other traits."

Dali gasped. The woman essentially found a way to make a shifter as vulnerable as a human.

"Traits?" she asked.

Megan shrugged. "No partial shifts, diminished senses, no telepathy."

She swallowed hard, trying to keep her heart from racing, remembering the role she was playing. "Oh my god." She faked a smile. "That is so cool. With this, we can take out every species we deem unworthy."

Megan's face lit up. "Yes, you understand me."

"Of course, I do. This blows my mind. You got anything to make women stronger than males or something?" For a moment, she felt lightheaded and wobbly.

From a box, Megan pulled out a syringe then stuck the needled into a jar with a milky substance inside. When she held up the full shot, Dali stepped back. Her instincts were screaming for her to get the hell out of there. But she couldn't not yet.

Megan laughed. "Don't worry. I'd never use this on you."

"What does it do?"

"Neurotransmitters," Megs said. "Wait till you see this. Stay awake for a bit longer."

Stay awake? Why would she say that?

Megan opened a door. "Turner bring the wolves out here." After Turner opened a door, she continued. "Everyone, follow Turner."

Turner? She'd heard that name recently, but her head was to foggy to remember. She leaned against the wall while men filed out of a room with a metal door and stood like statues. They looked normal, most in their factory jumpsuits still, until she studied their faces. Their unfocused eyes were creepier than shit.

"These are my wombies. Wolf zombies." Megan laughed, but she wanted to throw up. Instead, she forced a smile.

"What are they for?"

"These, my dear, are the beginning of our army. They are only responsive to my voice and will not stop until they have accomplished their tasks — which, of course, is to kill shifters and humans while they're at it." Meg straightened her back. "Everybody, shift now."

In seconds, a pack of wolves stood in front of

Dali. Her heart raced, horror coursing through her.

"They are ready to go," Meg said. "In a few minutes, I'll send them across the road to take out the rest of the pack, converting the other males there and take over their land."

Across the road? The pack was across the road? That's where she and Azai were before she woke in the ditch. Was Megan responsible for that? Did she have Azai? She tried to connect with her mate, but she felt the same lost link. She had to warn the pack about the wombie attack, but most of the men were in front of her. Then the answer hit her.

Valerie, do you hear me?

Yes, Alpha, where are you?

I don't have time to explain, please just do as I say.

Yes, Alpha.

Find Jed and get all the women across the road to the houses. Our missing men have been made into zombie-like killers set to take out the pack. You all have to stop them. Don't kill them since they're mates. Just find a way to keep them contained —

"Dalissa?" Megan's voice interrupted her wavering concentration. A hand gripped her arm. "Here, love. Sit down before you pass out."

Funny how Megan sounded like she knew

Dali was fighting sleep.

"Of course, I know," Meg replied.

Had she said that out loud?

"I'm the one who drugged your tea."

"Why?" Dali asked.

"Because you're perfect. I need your blood to make my DNA like yours."

Closing her eyes, Dali couldn't move. She heard Megan instruct Turner and someone else to bring out the prisoners. Prisoners? she wondered. Her mind was slipping away, but she thought she heard Azai yell her name. Then she was out.

TWENTY-SIX

Azai sat bound to his chair unable to get out of the steel cable holding him. This Megan knew what she was doing when it came to subduing shifters. But why would she go through all this trouble? What did she want?

The door opened and a man he barely recognized stepped in. "Turner?" he said. "My god, is that you?"

The man acted as if he'd not heard him.

Megan hollered from the other room. "Everyone, follow Turner."

The men were on their feet in a heartbeat and out the door. Only the sounds of their clothing rubbing floated in the room. They were drones, machines with no brains, the ultimate soldiers with shifter sense yet no sense to avoid death. That thought scared him. Someone with control over such creatures could cause a lot of trouble.

Turner returned to the room. This time with Nelda's husband, Harry. Turner unlocked the cable tying Azai's legs to the chair, then did the same for Remy. Azai thought of attacking, but his wolf was buried. He felt as weak as a human.

Turner grasped his arm and shoved him onto his feet as Harry did the same for Remy. When they stepped out the door, he saw the men had shifted to their four-legged forms. Then his heart crashed. His reason for living sat in a chair across the room, her head slumped onto her chest.

He yelled her name and tried to break free from his captor, but his effort was worthless. Turner smashed him to the floor to keep him under control.

"What have you done to her?" If he could shoot venom from his eyes, the bitch smiling at him would be covered in it.

"She's fine. Just sleeping," the woman replied.

"You lay one hand on her and I will kill you."

Megan laughed. "Aren't you so cute. So

protective. Too bad the only killing you will do is what I command." The bitch scooped up his unconscious mate and laid her on a metal table not far from him. He watched as Megan pulled medical supplies from a storage cabinet. On the table, she set a rubber tourniquet and a small needle connected to clear tubing that drained into a plastic bag.

"Why are you taking a blood sample?" he asked.

"I'm not taking a sample," she said as she wrapped the rubber band around his mate's upper arm. "I'm taking it all."

That set him into struggling against his captor, once again, to no avail. "What the fuck for? She's done nothing to you. She doesn't even know you."

Megan turned to him. "Take comfort in knowing that your mate was the perfect sacrifice to start our dream to a better world."

Rage, confusion, abhorrence, and grief rolled through him, overwhelming his mind. His hands fisted into balls as he tried to summon his wolf. Without his animal, he was useless against shifters. But he wouldn't give up. He'd fight to the death for Dalissa.

The psycho bitch stuck the needle in Dali's arm and the tube filled with a dark red liquid racing toward the bag hanging from the table's side. He watched as she took a small vial from the collecting container. A sample of his love's life source.

She inserted a needle into the capped end and drew out enough to fill it over halfway. Then she tapped her tapped at the vein in the crook of her elbow.

"Are you crazy?" Azai hollered. "You can't just put someone else's blood in your body? What's that going to do?"

Megan growled and hitched up the side of her top lip. "Her blood will become mine and I will have the supershifter abilities she has."

"Seriously? You think that will happen?"

She smiled. "I know it will."

Outside, a howl rang through the field. Jed. He was here? Then a female's cry followed his. Valerie?

Megan moved the blanket covering the windows at the back of room. "What the fuck is that noise?" She stood staring out then turned and slammed the syringe on the counter. "Turner, stay where you are. Everybody else follow me."

She stomped out of the room, his wolves following her like the Pied Piper. He heard a door open. He heard Jed's voice but couldn't make out the words. He appreciated his shifter senses all the more now that he experienced life without them.

He leaned toward Dali on the table. "Dalissa, wake up, baby. You've got to stop what this psycho bitch is doing to you." With no response, he pulled harder against Turner's iron grip. "Dali, love, hear my voice. Fight whatever drug she gave you."

Outside, Jed and Megan verbally sparred. Numerous growls erupted. How many wolves were out there? Sounded like half the pack. Then Megan's voice echoed. "Kill all the enemy!"

Shit. He turned back to his mate. "Listen to me, lioness, do whatever you need to, to wake your host. If you don't, Dalissa and you will die along with me and her entire pack. Get her awake."

Megan came back into the room, her heels clapping against the wood floor.

"Turner, get him away from her." She kicked a chair to the middle of the room. "Set his ass there and keep him quiet." She looked around. "Now, where were we?" She checked the blood bag which was almost full. She switched it out with an empty one. With a sigh, Megan picked up a syringe filled with a white liquid.

"All right, Alpha. Time for you to join your pack outside. You will do what I say when I say with no questions." She held up the needle and tapped the side to move air bubbles to the top then squirted them out.

Azai saw his mate's head turn. "I wouldn't move if I were you, Megan."

Dali sat up, pulling the needle from her arm. "It's time to stop this crazy ass stunt of yours."

Megan stepped back. "How are you awake? I gave you enough drug to down a male elephant."

Dali smiled. "I'm perfect, remember. My blood filters out toxins quicker than yours. Privileges of being pure blood."

"Pure blood?" Megan whispered. "Impossible."

"Not where I'm from. Now put down the needle."

An evil smile grew on the bitch's face. "Sure, I'll put it down. In your arm."

Azai watched as Megan, with shifter speed, lunged at his mate. But his mate was perfect and faster. With a hand shift, Dali swiped her paw through the air, slamming into Megan's arm, sending the syringe flying toward him. The needle flipped around to jab solidly into his thigh.

TWENTY-SEVEN

In her mind, Dalissa felt her cat dragging her consciousness up from a deep well. Her heart was pumping hard and fast to clean the toxin from her blood. She heard dog fighting outside, smelled her mate, and noted something in her arm. Then came Megan's voice. The bitch wanted to make her mate into one of those damn *wombies*. Over her freakin' dead shifter body.

She'd always taken the stand for peaceful resolutions. Walking away from trouble when she could. Thus, other seeing her as weak. But sometimes, that just didn't work. Then it was time to fight.

After batting away the needle from Megan's hand, she fully shifted and sprang for the woman.

Unfortunately, the bitch was ready for the change and was fast herself.

Dalissa charged, mouth open, forcing Megan into a table of equipment. Microscopes and beakers crashed to the floor. Back on her haunches, Megan swiped a claw-tipped paw across Dali's snout then launched at her. The two bit at each other, locking jaws together. Dali rolled onto her back and swiped up at the other lioness's neck, tearing away slashes of fur and skin.

Megan leapt back and swished her tail side to side, head lowered, pacing. Dali got to her feet, trying to keep herself between her mate and the enemy. Megan faked a lunge and Dali swatted her face, drawing blood. When Megan moved away, Dali stood her ground with her mate behind her. She was ready for everything except what happened next.

Megan shifted and yelled, "Turner, squeeze your alpha's throat so he can't breathe."

She swung around to see her mate struggling against the shifter's strangle hold. She was sure Turner was a nice person, but he had to die now. Dali jumped toward him to take him down, but out of nowhere, Megan slammed into her side, sending them both rolling into more tables and crashing equipment.

They tore at each other, paws scraping,

cutting, gashing at the other's head and neck. All the while, Dali kept her mate in her peripheral vision. He wasn't able to get free with his arms still tied behind him. He was going to die.

Dalissa sprang away and shifted. "Okay, I give. Let him breathe." Turner didn't budge. Dali yelled at the bitch, "Let him breathe!"

"Turner, loosen your hold." She then turned to Dali. "Do you see what I see, girl?"

What? She looked over her mate. Then Dali saw it—the syringe lodged in Azai's thigh. The plunger hadn't been pressed. He wasn't infected yet. Her heart crammed into her throat. She was going to lose the love of her life if she didn't do as the bitch wanted.

"Pull it out, Megan, or you won't like the consequences."

The witch cackled like a hyena on steroids. "No. I don't play that game. You will do as I say and I'll let him be."

Dali had no choice. The lioness could instruct Turner at any second to do her dirty work.

"Fine," Dali said. "What do you want?"

"The rest of your blood."

Azai squirmed in his chair Turner had forced him onto. "No, Dali. Don't do—"

"Turner, squeeze." His hand wrapped around her mate's throat again. Azai's face turned red as he fought uselessly.

"Stop. All right." Dalissa stumbled to the table with tubing and bags.

"Turner, let him go and hold the woman in place." The shifter's arm moved away, and he came at her. Dali was fine with that. Azai leaned forward in the chair, gasping for breath.

"Dali," Azai breathed out, "don't. Not for me."

She couldn't hold back the anguish of seeing the man she loved in so much pain. She nodded. "Only for you. I love you."

Megan rolled her eyes. "How disgustingly sweet. Let's nip this in the ass right now." She stepped over to the alpha barely remaining in the seat and slammed her hand on the plunger.

Dali screamed but she didn't hear it over her pulse drumming in her ears. Turner's grip on her shoulders tightened, digging into her muscles to hold her there. She watched as Azai fell onto the floor, thrashing, and kicking, his screaming popping the veins out in his neck. Then he slowly quieted, lying still, but panting.

"Hear me, Alpha," Megs said. "You will obey my commands with no hesitation, no thought." He made no movement. "Now, shift."

Azai's body spasmed so his back arched painfully. Then he squeezed into a ball. His face was blood red and she was afraid he'd have a stroke, but he didn't shift. Was he fighting it?

Megan strolled around his body on the floor. "Interesting. I forgot I suppressed his wolf."

"You what?" Dali screamed. What did that mean? Would he die? Would he be a zombie with no other half?

Meg ignored her, studying the wolf on the floor carefully. Dali heard clothes tearing and glanced at her mate to see him finally shifting.

"Ah, there he goes." The lioness pointed toward the kitchen. "Alpha, join your pack outside and kill all the enemy."

Azai rolled to his feet, the metal cables falling away and trotted out of the room.

"Oh, god, no." Tears rained down Dali's face. She'd lost her reason for living. Her heart crushed. She no longer cared what Megan did with her. She'd gladly give all her blood to the bitch. As a memory hit her, Dali smiled bittersweetly to herself.

"Megan, have you tried my blood yet? Felt its effects?"

Her enemy's eyes widened. "Is that what will happen? I will become stronger, more powerful."

She shrugged. "I'm not a doctor. I have no idea."

Megan picked up the syringe filled with Dali's blood, eyeing it closely. "I should test it first."

She laughed. "What for? Shifter blood is shifter blood. It's not like I'm from a different planet or anything."

Megan stared at her. The crazy shone in the woman's eyes. She was over the edge being so close to what she'd wanted for so long. "You're right," she said. "A little bit won't hurt."

Her ex-friend thumped the bend in her own elbow and inserted the needle, pressing the plunger. Dali held her breath.

Megan gasped and threw her head back. Moaning, she stumbled into the counter. "Fuck me, this feels great." In a couple breaths, she started wheezing and then she clutched at her chest. Megan doubled over, blood flowing from her mouth. She fell to her knees, scared eyes staring at her. "Turner, help me." She reached out for him.

The man released Dali and stepped toward the woman on the floor. He stood, doing nothing. Megan didn't know how to direct him. A mindless person was just a computer with no programming. All you got was a blank screen.

Megan's skin started to bubble up. The woman screamed as the flesh popped open, small pockets of blood squirting into the air.

Dali turned away, her legs no longer supporting her. Strong arms wrapped around her. She looked up to see Remy staring at the sight his ex-beta must've been at that point.

"Remy, you're okay. Where were you?"

"I was with Azai, tied up. When Megan said for everybody to go out and fight, she forgot to tell my captor to stay. He let me go and left with the others. Dumb move on her part. It took me some time to unlock the binding around my hands. Not sure if Turner did this on purpose, but he left the key on the floor next to the ankle shackles he unlocked." He looked around the room. "Where is Azai?"

"Oh, Remy, she turned him into a zombie with drugs like the others."

His horror-filled eyes met hers. Her heart broke all over again. "Where is he?"

"Outside with the others, fighting," Dali answered. The screaming behind her had quieted. She couldn't look.

"What happened to her?" Remy asked as they walked toward the kitchen.

"I'm not positive, but I think when she injected my blood into herself, it killed her."

"Did you know that would happen?" he asked.

"I didn't know what would happen. I just know our blood is poisonous to human blood. On our planet, we can't give blood transfusions between humans and shifters. Something about too much nitrogen needing to escape the blood."

"Sounds like the bends divers can get."

She nodded, not having a clue what he was talking about.

They reached the kitchen door where the fighting was on the other side. Remy pushed open the exit and they stood watching the battle. But battle wasn't the word she would've used.

She'd told Valerie not to kill the mates but subdue them. The scene was almost comical. There were at least two females for each male. One lady nipped at the male's tail, spinning them around, then the other female bit at his ass or legs, turning him around the rest of the way.

Several females wrestled the males to the ground but couldn't hold them down. The ladies weren't heavy enough to pin the males. They all needed to be a hundred pounds heavier.

But not every group was as tame.

Several injured wolves lay in the grass. She couldn't tell the degree of their injuries at this distance. But it didn't look like there were any deaths yet.

Dali looked around for Azai. She saw him fighting another huge wolf. It had to be Jed. Both were bloody and heaving for breaths.

Remy sighed. "If we can't find a way to stop them, especially your alpha, I'll have to kill him. You know that, right?"

Dali slapped her hands over her mouth to hold back the anguish escaping through her throat. She spun around, not able to stomach the thought of half her pack dying. Remy held on to her, rubbing her back.

He continued. "If only there was some kind of cure. I don't supposed Megan had some of that lying around?"

A cure? Dalissa's mind kicked into overdrive. Was it possible to counteract the compounds used? Megan had mentioned neurotransmitters. Dali didn't know anything about those, but she did know the chemicals used to create the synthetic concoction. If she could create a reversal, a cure. . .It was worth a shot.

Jed, Valerie. Keep everyone busy. I think I know how to get our loved ones back.

No problem, Valerie replied. *We're having fun!*

Speak for yourself, Jed commented.

Dali pulled away from Remy, heading back

into the house. She asked, "Do you know anything about human synaptic responses?"

Remy followed her inside. "You mean brain stuff? I have no clue, but google would know."

She glanced around the kitchen to see what gadgets were at her disposal. "Great. Who's google? Is he nearby?"

"Sure is." Remy pulled his phone from his pocket and pushed a button. "Hey, google. Tell me about synaptic responses." He stared at his phone for a second then handed it to her. "Here, I don't speak this language."

She took his phone, not understanding. Then she saw the first several words were medical in nature and each had over fourteen letters.

"This is great. I need to setup a chromatography analyses to see what the drug is made up of." She hurried into the room and grabbed the jar with the milky liquid and rushed out, trying not to look at the bloody body on the floor. Just the smell launched her into dry heaves over the sink.

Remy patted her back. "I'll clean up while you work on this."

She bobbed her head. "Thank you." Pulling herself together, she scanned her memories back to her school days and went to work.

***

Dalissa stared at the spinning machine in the kitchen. Quickly, it had separated the milky substance's compounds into their base parts. From there, she had to search the internet for transmitters and synaptic info. Now she was remixing, hoping to find a cure.

The fighting outside the door did nothing to calm Dali's nerves or improve concentration. She worried about her mate — killing and being killed. She worried about the pack members — mate against mate. And she worried that if she screwed this up, she could kill the pack herself. At least Remy had removed his beta's body from the main room.

Remy asked, "How's it coming?"

Dali plopped into a chair. "It's coming."

"Is there a hold up?" He sat beside her, leaning his elbows on the table.

"Well," she started, "I'm not sure if it's the γ-aminobutyric acid inhibiting the neurons or if the acetylcholine is interfering with the electronic transfer."

"I see," he said. "That's quite a conundrum. Would you like a piece of cheese?"

Dalissa laughed. The way Remy combined those completely different sentences was crazy. That or she was getting slap-happy — a term Zaria used when they'd had too much wine to drink and got silly stupid.

A buzzer went off, startling them both. The first attempt at a cure was ready for testing. "This has gone too smoothly," Dali said. "The compounds were easy to detect since they all smelled different. All the chemical were here, except one, which I had to make from scratch. And the battle outside is still raging, so not everybody is dead."

"I've kept an eye on it," Remy said. "It's the strangest thing I've ever seen. The male wolves are supposed to kill, but for the last thirty minutes they are hardly attacking the females. And the females are irritating the shit out of the males with their jabs and tail biting. But then there's Azai and Jed."

Dali stopped in the middle of the kitchen. "What about them?"

"They've both tired out but Azai hasn't backed down. He's still going after others and Jed has to fight him back. Some of the females have been helping by running circles around the alpha, making him fall over himself.

"Whatever Megan did, she didn't do it all that well. I thought they'd be unstoppable killing machines, but that's not the case." Remy shook his head.

"Guess she underestimated the power of the love between mates," Dali replied. "Even when out of their minds, the males know they have a connection." That's how she felt about Azai, anyway.

She took the jar from the mixer and held it up to the light. "This is it. How do we test it?"

They both leaned forward, looking through the cased opening into the living room where Turner stood exactly where he was when Megan died.

"Yup," she said.

"Agreed," he replied.

From a box, Dali pulled out an empty syringe, filled it with the new solution, and wrapped her hand around it like it was a knife handle. "You ready?" she asked.

Remy looked at her with concern on his face.

"What?" she asked.

"Have you ever given a shot before?" he questioned.

"No. Why?"

"I guess you don't watch any of those med dramas on TV?"

"No. We don't have TVs on Aurora. Am I doing it wrong?"

He held his hand out. "May I?" She gladly passed it over to him. He held up the syringe, needle to the ceiling, flicked it and pushed the plunger until it seeped out the end.

"Oh," she said. "Good thing I'm not a doctor. Go on and stick him. I think I'll throw up if I have to do it."

Remy raised the needle to Turner's upper arm and poked it through the skin. Turner didn't even flinch. Next, he injected the serum. Both stood back, waiting for something to happen. After a minute of no response, Dali's heart sank. If this first batch didn't work, she didn't know what she'd do. This was all she knew. Anything more advanced was over her head.

Just when she was going to schlepp back into the kitchen, Tuner grabbed his head and screamed, falling to his knees. He howled and grinded his teeth together, staying tucked in a ball. After a moment, he stopped moving.

Dali looked at Remy. She was sure the man was dead. Then he rolled over.

He said, "Who are you and where am I?" He sniffed at himself. "Shit. I stink."

Dali grinned. "It's been about three months since you bathed last." She grabbed the box of needles and hurried into the kitchen. She filled each then handed them to Remy. "You ready?"

"More than. Let's go."

When they stepped outside, a bizarre scene greeted her. Wolves were gathered into two main groups. The men were bunched together with the women forming a circle around them.

Okay, ladies. We have a cure. We just need to get close enough to inject each.

She and Remy stepped into the circle and received several growls for their effort. One leapt at her, catching her off guard. Flying in from the side, a female tackled the attacker, rolling him to the ground. The fight was back on.

Sorry 'bout that, Alpha, Valerie said. *Steve's a dick in or out of his animal.*

We have to hold the guys down to do this.

We've tried that, Alpha. We're not big enough. The buck us off every time.

"Remy," she said, "we can't do this. How do we get them to let us close?" They would have to kill their mates and friends. Then a loud roar came from the tree line.

One of the biggest lionesses Dali had ever seen stepped from the forest. She roared again as more filed out behind her.

Remy laughed. "Old Bertha said she's as pissed as a rattlesnake that we didn't include them in this party."

Dali snorted. "Not my kind of party."

Remy pointed and the pride split up, females coming closer. The men standing nearby. "Problem solved."

Dali watched as the lady wolves got the men to the ground, then the lionesses lay on top of each male, holding them down. The guys scrabbled and kicked, but they weren't able to touch the golden cats across their midsections.

Dali laughed at the situation. She was sure the men didn't find it quite as hilarious as the ladies did.

All the wolves were given injections except for the biggest. Jed and Azai had called a silent draw for the moment, both beat up badly. Remy held her back when they approached Azai.

"Let me do this. I might have to shift." Several of the lions had gathered to protect their alpha from the wolf alpha.

"No, Remy," she said. "He will force you to fight to the death and I won't have that for either of you. I'm his mate. If I can't pull this off, then no one can." She swallowed hard. "If I go down, do what you have to, to preserve lives." He handed the injection to her and she stepped past Jed.

There was a time to fight and a time for peace. Right now, her soul yearned for her mate and the bond that had been destroyed. She'd get him back or die trying.

"Hey, Azai. Looking pretty rough there, babe." A growl rumbled from his body as he paced. His eyes were feral, no sign of the intelligent man she knew to be trapped in the body. "Need you to do something for me. Think back to last night. Can you do that? Can you remember us zipping along the top of the world in the beauty of nature?

"Do you remember what you said to me when we watched the sun set fire to the sky? Think back, babe. Those memories are there. You just have to find them."

The alpha wolf stood in one place, staring at her. She stepped closer. "I'm your mate. Your true mate. I know you feel it. Search for our connection, feel my bite on your shoulder. It's there. Remember when we mated?"

The alpha shook his head side to side as if trying to dislodge a troublesome hat.

"I love you, Azai, and you love me. Love is the strongest thing in the universe. It unites souls from one galaxy to another, from one lifetime to the next. I want to spend the rest of our lives raising our pups in the pack. Teaching them how to be good mates and spoiling the grandcubs."

She stepped closer. If this didn't work and Azai chose to attack, then this would be her farewell speech to the world. "Azai, babe, I need you to lie on the ground and let me give you the cure to the sickness you have. You will come back to me then and we can get on with our lives."

Dali checked on how close the other lions were to her and her mate, then whispered, "And if you don't lie down this instant, I will take my clothes off right now and Jed will see me butt naked. What do you think about that?"

Azai roared and fell onto his stomach. Remy and the others darted in to hold him down in case he changed his mind. She held him tightly when the cure kicked in, reactivating the synaptic exchanges that the drug had to prevent from working, cutting off all logical thought.

When he was cured, he wrapped her in his arms, both lying on the ground. He said into her ear, "You're a funny girl, my love. I'm going to spank you when we get home."

She smiled. "Promise?"

TWENTY-EIGHT

After a long pow-wow in the field across the road from the pack land, everyone was up to date on what happened with Megan, her experimenting, and the cure. The lions knew about their ex-beta and were glad to see her ploys stopped permanently.

Dali and Azai trudged into the house, life barely remaining in her body after this day. When she heard her communicator ringing, she rushed upstairs to answer it.

Gerri Wilder's image popped up. "You are not going to believe what your parents did."

Dali could only imagine. She wouldn't put anything past them. "What now?"

"They hired a Karrax to scare you into coming back home."

"A Karrax?" Dali said. "There are Karrax on Earth?" Then the most important part of Gerri's statement hit her. "To scare me into going home? Seriously?" Dali balled her hands into fists. This was even low for her parents.

"He was the one outside my apartment. I'm sure he sent those notes to you. You need to go somewhere safe until he's caught," Gerri said.

"What does he look like?" she asked.

Gerri gave her the description of the alien, which sounded familiar to someone she'd recently seen. "And if your parents had done research first, they would've found that he was wanted for assault on his planet. He could hurt you, Dalissa. That's why you need to find a place he can't get to you."

"Wait, Gerri," she replied. "He's dead already. One of the lion pride got him."

"Really?" Gerri relaxed, her shoulders lowering. "Well, thank goodness for that. I was going to send my men after him."

"How about you send them after my parents. They could've really screwed this up for me."

Gerri sighed. "Yes, they could have. But we'll deal with that later. I need a drink after all this. We'll talk later, darling." Gerri cut the transmission and Dali walked down the stairs.

"Everything okay?" Azai asked.

"Sorta," she answered, dragging fingers through her hair. "I'm going to take a shower and go to bed."

Azai walked behind her close enough she felt his body heat against hers. "We can shower together later, now I need to have you. I could've lost you today and I need to feel your pussy wrapped around my cock. I need the closeness we can only achieve when completely connected."

Dalissa groaned and rushed up the stairs, dropping her clothes as she climbed. She raced through the bedroom door and climbed onto the bed. "Come on, slow poke, I'm ready and willing forever."

Azai walked in, his clothes gone from shifting earlier. "Forever isn't long enough, my love."

He lowered himself onto the edge of the bed between her legs and groaned. Air rushed in and out of her lungs, keeping her barely able to function. She looked down, watching him gaze at her drenched white lace thong. He grabbed the bit of lace between his fingers and pulled. A soft tear later and cool air caressed her pussy lips.

A whimper, soft and filled with need,

skidded past her lips. He raised his face to look at her.

"Azai..." She didn't know what to say, only that if he stopped now, she might go crazy. And kill him. Definitely kill him for teasing her.

His lip curled into a sexy, self-assured smile. He lowered his head and took a slow lick before she could process his words. "Mmm," he growled into her pussy. The vibration sent a wave of pleasure cascading through her. She dropped back on the mattress, holding the sheets in a white-knuckle grip.

"Oh my--"

He licked her pussy, around her clit, and down to her anus.

Fire lanced from her belly to down between her legs. "God!"

Azai licked her entrance, thrust his tongue into her pussy, and proceeded to fuck her with it. She moaned loudly. He tightened his arms around her thighs to keep her from squeezing at his head. In and out. Over and over, he propelled the raspy length of his tongue into her pussy.

Dalissa released the blanket bunched in her fists and grabbed the soft strands of his hair with both hands. She ground her sex into his mouth, rocking her hips over his lips.

"Oh, oh, oh, oh!" she moaned, turning her

focus solely on the winding tension inside her.

He rubbed two digits on her dripping entrance, plunged the fingers inside, and fucked her in quick, harsh moves. He flicked his tongue over her clit, licking small circles over the swollen nub. He twirled his ring finger over her wet ass and slid the wet digit in. Then he fucked her with two fingers in her pussy and one in her ass. She gasped, the tension drawing much tighter inside her.

Azai sucked the small pleasure center into his mouth and grazed it with his teeth in a light bite. She whimpered. She was so close. Azai sucked down on her clit. Dali screamed when a rush of pleasure traveled through her body. She panted air into her lungs, hoping to catch her breath.

Thick muscles corded his lower body, and his long, hard cock pointed straight up between his legs.

She opened her legs wide for him, and he shook his head in a negative.

"Get on your stomach," he said, his voice was a deep growl. The harsh tone only served to make her need rise all over again. His jaw was clenched tightly, and his nostrils flared. It was clear he was having a hard time controlling himself. For some reason, instead of being scared, she became more aroused.

Gingerly taking her time, she flipped onto her stomach, lifted her ass into the air, and smiled back at him. "Is this what you want?"

She watched him stroke the long length of his cock. Moisture gathered at the head, and he used it to lubricate himself.

He stepped close behind her, gripped her hips, and rubbed the head of his cock between her cheeks then slid the head of his cock down until he was at her entrance.

Azai groaned and then drove forward, filling her in one quick glide.

"Oh, my goodness." She dropped her head forward, her forehead resting on the soft sheets and her hands gripping the bedding.

He withdrew until he was almost completely out of her, and slammed in. She moaned, grasping the sheets tighter. His cock slammed in and out of her pussy in quick, fluid moves. His grip on her hips tightened.

The sound of flesh slapping flesh mixed with her loud moans and his groans filled the early evening air. With each hard thrust into her, he pushed her closer to her climax. His moves increased in speed and became more forceful. She wasn't sure what changed, but savageness took over his drives.

A powerful jackhammering from behind

had her seeing double. He growled, dropped over her back, his moves still faster, harder, and with a growing desperation. Bursts of heat rushed down her spine, through her body, and centered at her womb. His rough breaths and low growls sounded at the back of her neck, a harsh panting in sync with her own ragged breathing.

"Please, god, please..." She was ready to offer him everything if he'd just make her come.

Perspiration covered both their bodies, making it easier for him to slip and slide up and down her back. He brushed his lips over the bend in her shoulder, a slow flutter over her flesh before flicking with his tongue.

"I know what you want, baby. I know what you need." He licked her sweaty shoulder repeatedly, his raspy tongue adding to the overly sensitized feeling of her skin. "I'm going to give it to you right now, sweetheart."

Desperate moans rushed past the dryness in her throat. He pounded her with his cock. Her pants increased with each fluid stroke. His licks drugged her into such frantic desperation, she thought nothing of his teeth grazing her back.

"You're so fucking perfect, Dalissa." Her breath hitched, and her orgasm rushed toward her so fast, she could taste it.

Azai collapsed on the bed next to her and

tucked her against his chest. "So, I was thinking we could call our first girl Nala." Azai started to laugh and Dalissa propped her head up on his chest.

"Should I assume this is another Lion King joke? You really need to let me watch this movie."

"If I have my way, we are going to spend the next month educating you on classic lion movies and having lots of mind-blowing sex. And far, far, away from lunatics who want to keep you. You're my heart and I won't ever let you go."

EPILOGUE

"Ms. Wilder? We have a delivery for you. Should we send them up or hold it at the front desk?"

"Hmm, I wasn't expecting anything. You can send them up, thank you." A few moments later, she heard footsteps coming down the hall. She opened the door and all she could see was fruit in cellophane.

"Ms. Wilder, I have a fruit basket here for you from a Dali and Azai. Would you sign here please?"

Gerri laughed and signed her name. "Thank you very much."

She walked inside with her gift and set it on

the table. This was a very sweet gift, and they included a note!

Dear Gerri,

We wanted to thank you for setting us up, even when we weren't expecting it. If you're so inclined, Remy mentioned wanting to chat with you and if I recall, you said something similar. One request: Don't make it easy on him.

Love,

Dali and Azai.

Ah, yes. Remy Leandros, the lion pride king. Yes, Remy deserved to sweat a bit. This could be a fun match.

THE END

ABOUT THE AUTHOR

New York Times and USA Today Bestselling Author

Hi! I'm Milly Taiden. I love to write sexy stories featuring fun, sassy heroines with curves and growly alpha males with fur. My books are a great way to satisfy your craving for paranormal romance with action, humor, suspense and happily ever afters.

I live in Florida with my hubby, our kids, and our fur babies: Speedy, Stormy and Teddy. I have a serious addiction to chocolate and cake.

I love to meet new readers, so come sign up for my newsletter and check out my Facebook page. We always have lots of fun stuff going on there.

Find out more about Milly Taiden here:

Email: milly@millytaiden.com

Website: http://www.millytaiden.com

Facebook: http://www.facebook.com/millytaidenpage

Twitter: https://www.twitter.com/millytaiden

If you liked this story, you might also enjoy the following by Milly Taiden:

Sassy Mates / Sassy Ever After Series

Scent of a Mate *Book One*

A Mate's Bite *Book Two*

Unexpectedly Mated *Book Three*

A Sassy Wedding *Short 3.7*

The Mate Challenge *Book Four*

Sassy in Diapers *Short 4.3*

Fighting for Her Mate *Book Five*

A Fang in the Sass *Book 6*

Also, check out the **Sassy Ever After World on Amazon**

Or visit http://mtworldspress.com

Nightflame Dragons

Dragons' Jewel *Book One*

Dragons' Savior *Book Two (coming soon)*

Dragons' Bounty *Book Three (TBA)*

A.L.F.A Series

Elemental Mating *Book One*

Mating Needs *Book Two*

Dangerous Mating *Book Three*

Fearless Mating *Book Four*

Savage Shifters

Savage Bite *Book One*

Savage Kiss *Book Two*

Savage Hunger *Book Three*

Drachen Mates

Bound in Flames *Book One*

Bound in Darkness *Book Two*

Bound in Eternity *Book Three*

Bound in Ashes *Book Four*

Federal Paranormal Unit

Wolf Protector *Federal Paranormal Unit Book One*

Dangerous Protector *Federal Paranormal Unit Book Two*

Unwanted Protector *Federal Paranormal Unit Book Three*

Deadly Protector *Federal Paranormal Unit Book*

Four (Coming Soon)

Paranormal Dating Agency
Twice the Growl *Book One*
Geek Bearing Gifts *Book Two*
The Purrfect Match *Book Three*
Curves 'Em Right *Book Four*
Tall, Dark and Panther *Book Five*
The Alion King *Book Six*
There's Snow Escape *Book Seven*
Scaling Her Dragon *Book Eight*
In the Roar *Book Nine*
Scrooge Me Hard *Short One*
Bearfoot and Pregnant *Book Ten*
All Kitten Aside *Book Eleven*
Oh My Roared *Book Twelve*
Piece of Tail *Book Thirteen*
Kiss My Asteroid *Book Fourteen*
Scrooge Me Again *Short Two*
Born with a Silver Moon *Book Fifteen*
Sun in the Oven *Book Sixteen*
Between Ice and Frost *Book Seventeen*

Scrooge Me Again *Book Eighteen*

Winter Takes All *Book Nineteen*

You're Lion to Me *Book Twenty*

Also, check out the **Paranormal Dating Agency World on Amazon**

Or visit http://mtworldspress.com

Raging Falls

Miss Taken *Book One*

Miss Matched *Book Two*

Miss Behaved *Book Three*

Miss Behaved *Book Three*

Miss Mated *Book Four*

Miss Conceived *Book Five (Coming Soon)*

FUR-ocious Lust - Bears

Fur-Bidden *Book One*

Fur-Gotten *Book Two*

Fur-Given Book *Three*

FUR-ocious Lust - Tigers

Stripe-Tease *Book Four*

Stripe-Search *Book Five*

Stripe-Club *Book Six*

Night and Day Ink

Bitten by Night *Book One*

Seduced by Days *Book Two*

Mated by Night *Book Three*

Taken by Night *Book Four*

Dragon Baby *Book Five*

Shifters Undercover

Bearly in Control *Book One*

Fur Fox's Sake *Book Two*

Black Meadow Pack

Sharp Change *Black Meadows Pack Book One*

Caged Heat *Black Meadows Pack Book Two*

Other Works

Wolf Fever

Fate's Wish

Wynter's Captive

Sinfully Naughty Vol. 1

Don't Drink and Hex

Hex Gone Wild

Hex and Kisses

Alpha Owned

Match Made in Hell

Alpha Geek

HOWLS Romances

The Wolf's Royal Baby

The Wolf's Bandit

Goldie and the Bears

Her Fairytale Wolf *Co-Written*

The Wolf's Dream Mate *Co-Written*

Her Winter Wolves *Co-Written*

The Alpha's Chase *Co-Written*

Contemporary Works

Mr. Buff

Stranded Temptation

Lucky Chase

Their Second Chance

Club Duo Boxed Set

A Hero's Pride

A Hero Scarred

A Hero for Sale

Wounded Soldiers Set

If you enjoyed the book, please consider leaving a review, even if it's only a line or two; it would make all the difference and would be very much appreciated.

Thank you!

Printed in Great Britain
by Amazon